THE RASPBERRY RULES

Karen McCombie's Scrumptious Books

Sadie ROCKS!

Happiness, and All That Stuff
Deep Joy, or Something Like It
It's All Good (In Your Dreams)
Smile! It's Meant to be Fun

Collect all 16 fabulous titles!

7 sunshiney, seasidey, unmissable books

And her novels
Marshmallow Magic and the Wild Rose Rouge
An Urgent Message of Wowness
The Seventeen Secrets of the Karma Club

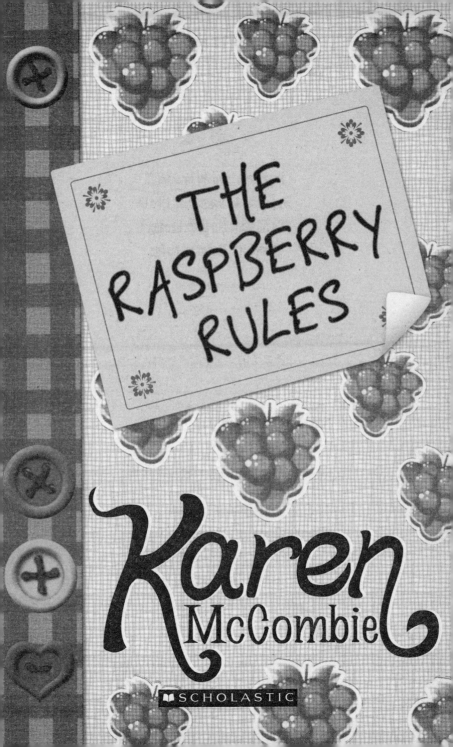

THE RASPBERRY RULES

Karen McCombie

SCHOLASTIC

First published in the UK in 2010 by Scholastic Children's Books
An imprint of Scholastic Ltd
Euston House, 24 Eversholt Street
London, NW1 1DB, UK
Registered office: Westfield Road, Southam, Warwickshire, CV47 0RA
SCHOLASTIC and associated logos are trademarks and/or registered trademarks of Scholastic Inc.

ISBN 978 1407 11553 5

A CIP catalogue record for this book is available from the British Library.

Printed in the UK by CPI Bookmarque, Croydon, Surrey.
Papers used by Scholastic Children's Books are made from wood grown in
sustainable forests.

5 7 9 10 8 6

This is a work of fiction. Names, characters, places, incidents and dialogues are products of the
author's imagination or are used fictitiously. Any resemblance to actual people, living or dead, events
or locales is entirely coincidental.

www.scholastic.co.uk/zone

For Wilfred and Ing,
of the Ally Pally Garden Centre café
(my "second office", only with cake)

The Raspberry Rules

Rule No. 1: I will be a NEW, IMPROVED, NON-ANNOYING ME!

Rule No. 2: I will make myself lots of RULES, which I will stick to.

Rule No. 3: I will be MORE focused.

Rule No. 4: I will NOT ramble so much.

Rule No. 5: I will do MORE things for my family.

Rule No. 6: I will NOT discuss knickers (whether squirrelly or not) in front of the male species again.

Rule No. 7: I will ALWAYS finish what I start.

Rule No. 8: I will NOT be confusing.

Rule No. 9: I will NOT be an irritating friend.

Rule No. 10: I will NOT steal.

Rule No. 11: I will NOT put raspberries in soup.

Rule No. 12: I will NOT eat emergency sandwiches over my journal while reading it through.

Rule No. 13: I will NEVER put rubbish out while only wearing out-of-date pants and a tartan blanket. . .

Rule No. 14: I will be BRAVE!

Rule No. 15: I will try to have a MORE varied and cultured vocabulary.

Rule No. 16: I will NOT drop journals or other important documents in the bath.

Rule No. 17: I will look and act more NORMAL.

Rule No. 18: I will get myself a NEW best friend – preferably one who isn't easily annoyed or embarrassed. . .

WEEK I

SATURDAY

Saturday 5.35 p.m.

Greetings!

And welcome to my new journal!!

I went to WHSmith's today planning to buy some new glitter gel pens and a packet of Hula Hoops in their half-price sale, but instead I saw *this* reduced to £2.49 from £4.99 and decided it might be fun to have one. (My sister Ally writes in *her* journal all the time.)

I think I will start with some facts about me and my life. Then when I am an old lady of ninety-three or whatever, I can compare it to my life *then*. (Hello, me at ninety-three, reading this! Wonder if you still like sandwiches made with cake decoration sprinkles as a filling?)

OK... here we go:

My name is: Rowan Mercedes* Love.

My age is: Thirteen.

My parents are: Mike (who is my dad and is lovely and is a bicycle repair man) and Melanie (who doesn't live with us, but is travelling and working around the world, which feels sometimes strange but mostly cool).

Do I have any brothers or sisters? Linn is fifteen and not that keen on me, Ally is eleven and pretty nice, and Tor is five and very, very cute, even if he doesn't speak all that much.

Anyone else important in the house? Grandma, who is Mum's mum, and comes round most days to help out with us and the house and our mess (poor Grandma).

Do we have any pets? Lots. We have two dogs (Winslet and Rolf), four cats (Colin, Eddie, Frankie and Derek), and heaps of small things in cages and tanks in Tor's room (I've lost count).

My best friend is: Erin, since Year Seven (we're in Year Nine now).

Favourite food: White-bread sandwiches with cake decoration sprinkles as a filling. (So colourful! So crunchy!)

Favourite colour: Tea-rose pink, magnolia pink, cherry-blossom pink – mmm.

Hobbies: Making stuff, giving myself interesting hairstyles, thinking of new things to do with glitter.

Favourite subject at school: Art – especially craft stuff.

Favourite thing ever: Glitter, of *course*.

That was fun!

Right – think I'll go downstairs and get a pre-tea snack.

Will scribble some more interesting and dynamic stuff later. . .

---

* OK, so I'm not *really* called "Mercedes". But Mum and Dad just forgot to give me a middle name, so I sometimes like to try different ones out for size.

Saturday 5.15 p.m.

Hello again.

It's ten minutes since my last journal entry, and I am writing this under my duvet with a glitter gel pen (bronze) and a bat-shaped Halloween torch (it belongs to Tor).

The thing is, I'm hiding.

I *know* hiding in your own room isn't really a fantastic idea ("Where's Rowan? Oh, I'd better try her room first!"), but I panicked.

I panic a lot. I'm happy a lot too, but sometimes the

panicking can get in the way of the happiness and sort of trips it up.

Anyway, I was feeling pretty happy and positive today (you probably noticed), till I realized — *big-time* — that I'm annoying.

Well, *I* don't think I'm annoying, but over the last week or so, it's sort of occurred to me that I seem to have annoyed a lot of people. And downstairs in the kitchen, Dad is about to be the *next* person to be annoyed with me, and disappointed too, so that's why I'm hiding.

"WHAT?! YOU HAVEN'T SHOWN HIM YOUR *SCHOOL REPORT* YET?!" Linn yelled at me five minutes ago, when I was in the kitchen fixing my pre-tea snack.

Blah. She'd just spotted the envelope I'd hidden at the back of the bread bin.

"YOU'VE HAD THAT SINCE *TUESDAY*, RO!!" she yelled some more, flipping the report out and scanning it at high speed (i.e., before I could put down the tub of sprinkles and the scone I was holding and grab it from her).

Y'know, *technically*, my big sister didn't <u>actually</u> yell. In real life, she has this very low, quiet, very together sort of voice. In *every* way, Linn is very together and organized and neat and stuff, which is why I think she is allergic to me (I bring her mood out in a rash if I'm in the same room as her). And so whenever she talks to me, it sounds in my head like she's shouting for *sure*.

Anyway—

Saturday 6.05 p.m.

Sorry for the interruption.

That was Tor again, lifting the duvet up and sliding a Babybel cheese over towards me. He really is very sweet. He hasn't even *asked* me why I'm under here, just peeked at me and shoved stuff in that he obviously thinks might cheer me up/be useful.

So far, apart from the bat-torch and the cheese, he's brought me his favourite toy (Mr Penguin), a plastic pencil sharpener in the shape of a fossil, and his library book about earthworms.

Like I say, Tor's not exactly chatty. Which means I probably don't need to worry about him telling anyone that I'm here.

But forget about Tor for a second.

Let's get back to my big sister and my (gulp) school report.

While Linn was yelling (sort of) about it in the

9

kitchen, I heard the front door open, and there was Dad back from work, whistling and happy from a busy day fixing bits of broken bikes, and looking forward to a chilled-out Saturday evening hanging out with three lovely, non-annoying kids.

And *me*.

Yep, I was about to spoil his chilled-out Saturday evening with my ropey report. So I did the only reasonable thing I could, and ran upstairs to hide when I heard him "hello!!"-ing at Ally and Tor in the living room.

And of course by now, Linn will have *definitely* waved my stupid school report under his nose, and I bet that right at this second, Dad will be reading it and feeling a bit <u>glum</u>.

It's not that my teachers say I'm some out-of-control, gum-chewing, head-flicking, teacher-cheeking thirteen-year-old or anything. I mean, they always all say stuff like I'm nice or whatever. It's just that after every teacher's "*Rowan's nice*" comment there always comes a big, fat "*but. . .*"

It's like with Miss Howie. For *her* section of the report, she wrote: "*Rowan is an intelligent girl, but she finds it hard to focus*". I think this is because she found me sewing felt squirrels on a pair of knickers in her physics class.

Mr Svenson, who does modern studies, wrote: "*Rowan has a vivid imagination, but finds it hard to apply herself*". OK, so everyone else did that whole write-a-CV exercise as if it was a *real* CV with your *real* skills on it, and said stuff like how they wanted to be management consultants or geophysicists and had scout badges in making NASA-approved telescopes out of toilet-roll tubes or whatever.

Then there was *me*, assuming it was just a fun assignment, and so I put down "*Princess*" in the Job Description box, and listed my skills as "*glitter technician*" and "*being able to sew my own ball gown if necessary*" (with a funky, sort of punky ball gown design doodled beside it in silver gel pen).

Mr Jong in history said I rambled. Yeah, so I wrote 5,314 words for my 800-word homework on The Great Exhibition of 1851. But I thought he'd be *pleased*. I'd've thought that showed enthusiasm, rather than a bad case of rambling. . .

Miss Malkovich, the PE teacher, said she'd prefer me to concentrate on learning the rules of netball rather than accessorizing my team bib. (Kerise Bennett complained that the foil stickers I'd added to the number 9 dazzled her eyes and made her miss a shot.)

Then it was Mrs Wells' turn. Mrs Wells is my form teacher. She wrote that I was a *"joy of a girl, though try as she might, Rowan doesn't seem to GET rules"*. I kind of understand what that was about, but it wasn't really fair. I mean, I *know* that when the school bell goes, you're meant to jump up and go places straight away, but I have a condition of the brain (probably) where I genuinely don't register the sound of bells for at least two minutes after they've gone off.

Mrs Wells' comment was the first one Linn saw downstairs, when I was trying (and failing) to grab my report out of her hand. When I began to babble an explanation, she yelled, "THAT IS *NOT* A GENUINE BRAIN CONDITION, RO!!" and ranted on *again* about how I should have shown Dad my report *days* ago and informed me that I am an idiot.

!?!

It was all a bit harsh, but to be fair, I think Linn was annoyed with me already because I made a face when she mentioned she was doing Mexican food with roll-up pancakes for tea. I pulled a face because she always puts really hot salsa in the roll-up pancakes and it's so spicy it makes the top of my head feel like it's got a painful kind of sherbet fizzing going on in it. Whatever, Linn took great offence at my "oh-no-not-salsa!" face and said that I never appreciated <u>anything</u> she did. "AND MAYBE IF YOU TOOK YOUR TURN AND DID SOMETHING FOR THE FAMILY ONCE IN A WHILE, YOU'D HAVE THE RIGHT TO COMPLAIN, *RO*!!"

To rub it in, Linn added that Grandma had been moaning to her about the fact that I never finished anything I started. (I forgot I'd told Grandma that I'd take the washing in from the garden after school on Thursday. And I forgot that I'd left it in a nice pile on the garden bench, and so it all got a bit wet in the thunderstorm that happened in the night.)

Oh, and if *that* wasn't enough, APART from annoying my teachers (with my lack of focus and attention to rules, etc.), and annoying Linn (with face-pulling, and not doing enough around the house, etc.) and Grandma (for not finishing things I start), it turns out that my best friend, Erin, is annoyed with me too.

It's 'cause—

Saturday 6.20 p.m.
Sorry – Ally just came into my room.

"Are you all right, Ro?" I could *sort* of hear her saying in a muffled, distant way. "Tor came and whispered to me that you were hiding under here. . ."

Yeah, so Ally *would* be the one Tor would tell. I think

there must have been some mix-up somewhere in the order our family arrived, because Ally is *much* more mature and sensible than me, even though she is eleven, which makes her two years younger. (Like last week, she told me to calm down and helped tidy away the charred bits of paper when I accidentally read my magazine over the gas cooker and set fire to it.)

Anyway, I figured out that the reason Ally sounded a bit distant when she spoke just now was because I was curled up *upside down* under the duvet, and so she was (pretty understandably, I guess) thinking my bum was my head and talking to it.

I didn't say anything back, though. I just tore a strip of paper out of the middle of this journal and scribbled: "*I'm OK. Please leave me alone. xxx*", and wiggled it out in Ally's vague direction.

She took it, and then I supposed she'd left. But after a few seconds, the note came sliding back under the duvet, and I felt the vibration of Ally's footsteps pad out of the room.

I shone the bat-torch on the paper and saw she'd scrawled, "*OK. But if you decide never to come out, can I have your nail varnish collection? xxx*"

She's smart, my sister Ally, but she's also pretty funny.

You know something? Ally and Tor are probably the *only* people who aren't annoyed with me just now.

Which brings me back to Erin.

She's annoyed with me 'cause of the squirrel knickers.

Here's why: yesterday in class, Ben Davidson threw a scrunched-up piece of paper at me, and when I opened it up, it read, *"Are you wearing your squirrel knickers today?"*

And then Miss Howie did that teacher thing of saying, "What's so interesting that you're not paying attention to the lesson, Rowan?" and I had to explain that Ben wanted to know if I was wearing the squirrel knickers (the ones Miss Howie had caught me making last week, of course), but that I *wasn't* because they were <u>actually</u> a present for Erin.

I hadn't wanted to say that, because I still hoped they'd be a surprise for Erin's birthday in three weeks' time. (I'm not usually very good at planning ahead, but I decided to try with this present, since craft stuff can go horribly wrong, like the time I made my sister Ally a papier-mâché piggy bank and didn't wait for the gluey paste to dry before I wrapped it up in gift paper. . .)

The thing was, Erin wasn't too thrilled about me mentioning her surprise birthday squirrel knickers *either,* not because it ruined the surprise for her but because she was mortified at the idea of wise-guy boys like Ben and his mates knowing a) anything about what knickers she <u>might</u> or might <u>not</u> be wearing, and b) that she liked squirrels in the first place.

(Erin really is *mad* on squirrels. She might have posters of her favourite girl bands on her walls, but she also has three whole shelves of squirrel ornaments in her room at home and a soft toy squirrel called Sir Timothy Nutkins on her bed.)

Thinking about it, I'm pretty sure I really *will* stay under my duvet for ever – that way I can never annoy anyone *ever* again.

Ally will suit my pale, pearly-blue nail varnish.

Though she's *definitely* going to have to stop biting her nails. . .

Saturday 6.37 p.m.

I'm still under the duvet.

But even though I think I may be starting to suffer from heatstroke, I *have* just had an ILLUMINATING THOUGHT!!

I am going to use this journal as a *fresh start.*

Mrs Wells, my form teacher, is wrong – I *can* get rules!

There is going to be a NEW, IMPROVED, NON-ANNOYING ME! (That's the *first* RULE of my new, improved life.)

Rule No. 2: *I will make myself lots of RULES, which I will stick to.*

Rule No. 3: *I will be MORE focused.*

Rule No. 4: *I will NOT ramble so much.*

Rule No. 5: *I will do MORE things for my family.*

Rule No. 6: *I will NOT discuss knickers (whether squirrelly or not) in front of the male species again.*

Whoo-hoo! Six RULES already!

Oh, and I've got another one; one Grandma would approve of:

Rule No. 7: *I will ALWAYS finish what I sta—*

Saturday 6.49 p.m.

Sorry. Dad interrupted this time.

He came into my room, after knocking and calling out my name softly. (I held my breath and didn't reply.)

But somehow he knew I was there.

I mean, of course, I realize *now* that I probably looked like a large person-sized lump under a candy-pink duvet, but I do have lots (and *lots*) of cushions piled on my bed, and hoped maybe Dad would be fooled into thinking I was anywhere else but underneath the mound.

At first, it sounded like he was *panting*, till I heard and felt something scrabbling under the bed and realized Winslet must have come in with him. (Winslet has short enough legs for under-bed scrabbling. Rolf is *way* too big and gangly.)

"Honey, you really don't have to get yourself all wound up about your school report, you know," I heard Dad say, as he sat down on the bed.

He had to move to a better spot straight away – he'd plonked himself on the bat-torch.

I didn't say anything.

I even tried not to breathe, but it made me see purple and crimson spots, like a psychedelic version of the solar system swirling in front of my eyes, so I gave up and gasped some (hot) air in.

"Reading through . . . it's great! Well, *mostly* great!" Dad continued. "And I *know* you always do your best, Rowan."

Yes, I do. It's true.

But from now on, I'm going to do even *better*, he'll see. From now on, he'll be EXTRA proud of me, just like he's proud of Linn for her braininess, and Ally for her funniness and sensibleness, and Tor for being, like, practically a professor of zoology, even though he *is* only five.

I tried to tell Dad all that telepathically, through the duvet and cushion mountain. It was starting to get *enormously* hot under there, and I'd just stabbed myself in the thigh with the gel pen.

"Just promise me you won't hide things from me any more. OK?" came Dad's voice again.

OK, I told him telepathically, while I wondered if there was a certain temperature that you had to reach to make yourself self-combust.

Dad must have heard me, because he sort of patted me reassuringly through the duvet (he got my elbow) and I felt him get up to leave.

"Linn says tea will be ready in about half an hour, in time for *Dr Who*. All right?"

All right, I silently answered him.

As soon as he clicked the bedroom door shut, I threw the duvet off and *breatheddddddd*. . .

I think I must have sounded like a drowning person who makes it to the surface of the water, gasping for dear life, because Winslet started growling in alarm under my bed. She doesn't like shocks and surprises, especially when she's got a new toy to chew on (Linn's hairbrush, it turned out).

Saturday 9.17 p.m.

I ate all my Mexican wraps, and even added extra salsa, just to show Linn that I'm not ungrateful. I took two paracetamol for the fizzy headache I had after.

Dr Who was pretty scary, though Tor cried when the seven-metre-tall, man-eating alien insect thing was killed at the end. (He didn't cry at all when the seven-metre-tall, man-eating alien insect thing killed all the screaming people who were begging for mercy.)

Ally offered to serve up the ice cream we were having for pudding and she gave me the biggest bowlful, for sure. I think she knew my mouth was on fire and my head was melting, probably because steam was rising from my fringe.

Saturday 9.38 p.m.

But what are you meant to write in journals, exactly? I mean, I can't just write RULES in it. There are a lot of pages, and it would mean I'd have a journal with about seventy-thousand rules, and even though I am going to be a new, focused me who finishes what she starts and lives by rules, I think that might just be too many.

Saturday 9.52 p.m.

I've got it.

Ally is downstairs with everyone else, watching the end of our crummy old video of *Men In Black II*. (Tor was in the mood for more aliens. He fell asleep one minute into the opening credits, and Dad covered him up with the tartan blanket and Derek the cat.)

I'm going to sneak into Ally's room up in the attic and see what she writes in all HER journals. That will help me figure out what to do with mine.

I should be a spy. . .

Saturday 10.05 p.m.

I have no future career as a spy. I'm not very good at sneaking.

First, I tripped over Ally's mound of trainers; THEN I tripped over Rolf the dog, who was sleeping half on the mound of trainers.

THEN I thunked my head on the blow-up globe that dangles from the middle of the ceiling and squeaked in surprise, and THEN Ally – who was in bed early and *not* eating home-made popcorn downstairs and watching aliens being blown up – said, "What are you doing, Ro?"

Ally was very cool about me crashing into her room

and waking her up. Like I say, she is *always* very cool, *and* funny and nice to me. Anyway, she said her journals were private, but if I squinted my eyes all thin so that everything was blurry and I couldn't read the actual (private) words, she would hold up one of her journals and flip through it for me.

While she flipped and I squinted blurrily, she explained that she writes down what's happening with *her* and *us* and her *friends* and stuff, and how she's feeling (about herself and us and her friends and stuff, I guess).

I can do that.

My journal won't *all* be rules.

It'll be rules, and feelings, and instructions on how to make a butterfly hair clip, etc. That last bit was Ally's idea too.

"And you can sometimes write about craft stuff you're doing!" she suggested.

I think she was inspired to say that because of the flock of butterflies pinned to the right side of my head.

I accidentally came up with the butterfly flock because I was staring at this new journal earlier and stressing about what to do with it, and tied shiny Celebrations sweet wrappers around a nearby hairgrip without thinking, really.

I've just checked it out in the mirror. It looks excellent. I may make more. A whole flutter of them.

CRAFT INSTRUCTIONS

Sweetie butterfly clip
You'll need:
- 1 hairgrip
- Some sweets with shiny wrappers

Instructions:
1) Eat the sweets.
2) Knot sweet wrappers around the hairgrip.
3) Fiddle with wrappers till they look like wings.
4) Stick in hair.

SUNDAY

Sunday 4.01 a.m.

Wow. I woke up in the airing cupboard just now with THE most excellent idea about how to help my family more! (Rule No. 5, remember!)

And it's all because of Grandma's friend Patricia winning a hamper of German wine, bratwurst and gugelhupf (it's a cake) in a Christmas edition of her favourite magazine for old people.

It's not that I'm particularly envious of her winning the wine or the sausage (the gugelhupf sounded pretty nice, though); it's just that, well, our family is a tiny bit poor, right? (Right.)

So, if I enter a bunch of magazine competitions EVERY WEEK, I'm bound to win stuff for my family, aren't I?

Hey, get *me*, Linn! I'm not an idiot, I'm practically a genius!!!

Sunday 4.33 a.m.

I should really try to get back to sleep, but my head is still buzzing with possibilities. I could probably single-handedly win enough groceries and toiletries and treats and stuff to keep my family in luxury for life! How non-annoying would *that* be?!

By the way, how AMAZING is my secret sleepwalking? It doesn't happen very often, but when it does, I just love the thrill of waking up somewhere unexpected (like in the airing cupboard), usually with some very random dream or thought pinged right at the front of my brain.

(My personal favourite: the time I found myself standing in the kitchen, making a peanut-butter-and-washing-up-liquid sandwich, with an excellent idea for a new hairstyle, involving two plaits and some picture-hanging wire to make the plaits go bendy.)

My sleepwalking is all very secret, hush-hush from the rest of my family, of course. I mean, I've never told them about it. That's 'cause it started a couple of years ago, the same time as Tor started having nightmares, i.e., when Mum moved away abroad.

I keep it secret because Dad and Grandma might stress and think it was a symptom of *me* being stressed with not having Mum around, but a) I love my sleepwalking (it's like having a slightly useless superpower), and b) even though I *do* miss her, I think it's brilliant if Mum wanted to live and work in other countries and went and did it, instead of staying at home and suddenly finding she was eighty (which is in about forty years' time) and regretting never doing it.

My dream is that some day I could hang-glide over the Himalayas dressed as an angel. If I had a husband who said that was a nuts idea (as if), I'd do it anyway.

Sunday 5.15 a.m.
Argh.

Just thought of a problem with entering heaps of magazine competitions. Dad can't afford to give us much pocket money and magazines cost a lot.

Argh, argh, argh.

Sunday 11.55 a.m.
It's all OK!

I came downstairs a while ago for breakfast (fell asleep sometime after 6 a.m., woke up half an hour ago with the indentation of a glitter gel pen in my cheek), and guess what I saw in the paper-recycling bin in the kitchen?

Only the *HORNSEY JOURNAL*!! How excellent is that? The local newspaper that my grandma gets – without fail – every Friday! She always reads it here, while she's "babysitting" us after school and making tea.

Anyway, apart from articles about the outrage over new parking meters and the disgrace of teenagers loitering somewhere, it has – **IMPORTANT!! IMPORTANT!! IMPORTANT!!** – **COMPETITIONS** and **GIVEAWAYS** in it!!!

I immediately took my toast and the *Hornsey Journal* back up here to my bedroom and entered competitions to win:

- Anti-ozone air freshener
- Six packets of Wall's sausages
- A foot deodorizer set
- Subscription to *Your Health and You!* magazine
- A box set of World War II DVDs

Bring it on!!

Sunday 4.35pm
It just gets better.
DAD SAYS I CAN **PAINT** MY ROOM!!

The daisy wallpaper has been up there from when we first moved in (I was two) until now. It's very pretty, but sometimes, when I'm thinking about stuff, I find myself staring at it without realizing, and let me tell you, staring at all those hundreds of tiny daisies can give you a migraine, for sure.

Here's the thing. I was up at Alexandra Palace Park playing frisbee with Dad and Ally and Tor and the dogs this afternoon. (Erin was supposed to be coming to watch a film at mine, but when I phoned to see where she was, her mum said she'd had to go to the shops with her dad instead.)

Anyway, the grass was absolutely *heaving* with daisies and Tor said it was *exactly* like my wallpaper, and I made a face.

I panicked when I saw that Dad had seen me pull the face, because I knew Mum had specially chosen the wallpaper for me *way* back when I was small, and so I thought he might mind that I was wearing an expression like I might be sick.

But instead he said, "Getting a bit grown-up for all the flowery stuff, are you, Rowan, babes?"

And I nodded (I *was* going to answer "yes", but Tor caught me on the mouth with a rogue frisbee shot).

While Dad dabbed at my split lip with a tissue, he

reminded me that Linn got to redecorate *her* bedroom in the autumn, so it was only fair. (Her *old* wallpaper was off-white, with a matching off-white border with cream lilies on it. She then painted the whole lot bright white. Linn is not very radical when it comes to colour.)

So anyway, the daisies are HISTORY!!

Right now, I'm going to go and spend what pocket money I have left on stamps from the Turkish shop on Hornsey High Street, and send off all my competition entries. The blokes who run the Turkish shop are very smiley. Linn says it's because I'm usually wearing something ridiculous and they're laughing at me. She's just jealous 'cause when *she* goes in there, they don't smile at her at all. (She's scowled at them too many times.)

Then I'm going to go to Grandma's flat and see if she has a paint colour chart.

Grandma probably *will* have a paint colour chart. She is the most organized person I know (apart from Linn). If you open the third drawer down in her kitchen, there will be neat boxes of spare fuses and light bulbs and candles in case of power cuts.

If you open the third drawer down in *our* kitchen, you're likely to find a dog-eared copy of *Cycling Weekly* from 1998, a half-finished packet of hamster food, and Frankie the cat sleeping.

MONDAY

Monday 10.40 a.m.

I wasn't sure if I should take my precious new journal into school today, in case I was wildly unlucky and got mugged on the way or something. Not that it would have been very exciting for the muggers; instead of finding money or a mobile (I don't have either), they'd have got away with . . .

- this journal,
- the colour chart I borrowed from Grandma yesterday evening,
- a leftover felt squirrel that didn't make it on to Erin's knickers (looked too much like an owl), and . . .
- a fluffy something that might be a throat lozenge from when I had a cold back in February.

"I wouldn't worry," said Erin, while we hung out at

morning break. "There's no *way* muggers would be seen dead with *that!*"

I think she meant 'cause of the customizing I've done on my bag. It's just that I got all these old-lady beaded necklaces from the local charity shop and sewed them on to my bag, in sort of draping swathes (swathing drapes?).

Maybe Erin is right, but then maybe some muggers would be more open-minded to avant-garde artistic statements than she thinks. She can be quite narrow-minded.

"Why are you writing a journal anyway?" Erin asked me after that. (I'd pulled out a corner of my new book and showed it to her in Mr Svenson's class earlier.)

"Why not?" I shrugged back.

I like Erin a lot. She's been my best friend since the second day we started at Palace Gates School, when we both had to sit out PE with ice on our heads after crashing into each other during a game of hockey. I've always hated hockey but liked Erin since then.

But the thing with Erin is she always has to know WHY about stuff, like <u>why</u> we have four cats and not just one, and <u>why</u> I put different-coloured eyeshadow on each eyelid for the Christmas school disco, and <u>why</u> I made tiny curtains for Tor's gerbil cage.

The thing is, sometimes in life, there're just no answers. . . (Heard that at the end of a TV movie me and Ally watched one rainy Saturday afternoon recently. Good, isn't it?)

"So what shopping did you and your dad have to do yesterday?" I asked Erin, changing the subject. But there was no answer to that either.

"I'm hungry. Fancy a fruit bar from the vending machine?" she asked.

Uh, *hello*. . .! And people think *I'm* dippy! It was like she hadn't heard a word I was saying!

Whatever.

Actually, Erin's been gone a long time now — which is fine, because it gives me this chance to scribble some stuff in my journal. What's *not* so great is that it's made me worry that the machine's run out of fruit bars.

I may faint from lack of sustenance.

I may be forced to eat the fluffy throat lozenge at the bottom of my bag.

Monday 12.50 p.m.

Lunch was lovely (veggie lasagne). Was VERY hungry due to Erin failing to get fruit bars at break time (???). She said she ran into Ingrid and Yaz but then she couldn't remember what they were talking about.

(Probably the lack of food was affecting her concentration.)

Anyway, now that I've got time, here's some other interesting stuff from this morning...

- ASSEMBLY: This is normally quite boring. But today I was more focused and listened properly (for once), and I was glad I did, 'cause I found out that the girls' toilets on the ground floor are closed for repair (important when desperate for a wee, or if you want to avoid alarming startled workmen when you wander in, trying to rearrange an uncomfy bra strap).

  Also, our head teacher, Mr Bashir, introduced a new student teacher called Miss Boyle, who is young and very round and cheerful, with teeny little doll feet in kitten heels. She has a short brown bob, and was wearing a top as red as her lipstick and a brown suede skirt. She looked *exactly* like a robin. (I like robins.)

- LIBBY-MAE FERGUSON IN YEAR ELEVEN HAS A VERY CUTE NEW HAIRDO: Libby-Mae Ferguson is in Linn's year, but they're not friends or anything. (Linn just mooches around and looks serious with her best friends. From what I can see, Libby-Mae is more of a hanging-out-and-giggling-with-her-mates kind of girl, which is *way* too frivolous for Linn.)

Anyway, I've always thought Libby-Mae Ferguson looked kind of pretty and nice and everything, but when I saw her queueing at the salad bar today, I noticed she'd done this absolutely *different* thing. It's like, in our school, most of the girls sign up for one of two hairstyles available; i.e., the pulled-tight, low-slung ponytail (Linn's hairdo of choice), or the Alice band with floppy fringe (Erin and Ingrid and Yaz and about a zillion other girls go for that one). There's practically only me and Zoe Clark in Year Seven that have anything remotely different. Me, 'cause I do things like tie mine up, and sometimes tie stuff *into* it, and Zoe Clark 'cause her mum always cuts it into this drastic pageboy style that makes Zoe look permanently alarmed.

But now Libby-Mae has ditched her Alice-band-with-floppy-fringe look, and has let her long, auburn hair float free, but looking all crinkle-cut-chip effect, like she's had it in loads of tiny plaits all night. It's *excellent.*

· ERIN'S DAD CAN TAKE ME TO BUY PAINT!: "He's got to go to the paint shop later today – he'll pick us

34

up from school," Erin had told me, when she read her dad's text.

Erin's dad Dave is a plumber, which is cool, because he can take me to the trade centre place he goes to, which sells plumber-y and paint stuff to plumbers and painters *only*, and can get a big discount for me.

Oh, and Dad gave me £20 towards paint last night. Yay! (Sadly, *he* can't take me to buy the paint himself because it's quite a long way to the regular DIY store and he wouldn't be able to carry me AND a two-litre pot of paint on the back of his push bike.)

Now I just have to choose a colour. I'm going to go for a shade that is mature and serene, in keeping with the new, improved, non-annoying me.

I'm looking through the "Whispers" range from Crown. They are called things like "A Whisper of Snowfall" and "A Whisper of Mellow Sage" and "A Whisper of Pashmina".

Just the very *names* are making me feel very calm and non-annoying.

Monday 5.47 p.m.
Oooh, my new paint colour is delicious, DELICIOUS, DELICIOUS!!

"Wait a minute," said Ally, when I opened the pot downstairs to let everyone see.

She ran out into the hall and then came back in wearing Tor's Tigger sunglasses.

Tor didn't mind. He just started jumping about singing "Ra-Ra-Raspberry!!" (the name of the paint colour).

Dad grinned and said "Wow!!" when he saw it.

Grandma shrugged and muttered something about it being quite jolly, she supposed.

Linn yelled "IT'S DISGUSTING!", which is a bit much for a girl who lives in a room that's decorated like the inside of a fridge.

Rolf must have thought my Ra-Ra-Raspberry was delicious too, 'cause I had to stop him licking it.

The trade centre paint shop was fun, by the way. (Erin wouldn't come in – she sat in her dad Dave's van the whole time flicking through a copy of *Bliss* magazine.)

"Don't think they get a lot of schoolgirls who look like you in here!" Erin's dad Dave said, nudging me, like I didn't already notice that about twenty plumber- and builder-type blokes were staring at me. You'd think an ostrich in Ugg boots had just walked in. I mean, I was in my school uniform, so big wow!! (Perhaps it was the sweetie wrapper hairgrips that did it. That and my pink, silver and purple over-the-knee socks, maybe.)

One of the guys who worked there was the best. Erin's dad Dave got talking to him and said I was choosing some paint. The guy took one look at me and pointed over to a bunch of pots and said, "Checked out the sale stuff, love?" in a gruff voice.

And there it was — my Ra-Ra-Raspberry, in between strange, unsellable shades of faint grey and dog-poo brown gloss.

For (get this) only a **fiver**!!

I now have <u>vats</u> of money left over to buy gorgeous room accessories.

Where can I buy a giant mirrorball, do you think?

Monday 7 p.m.

Grandma is in a slightly bad mood with me, as nobody noticed Rolf padding off from the open tin of Ra-Ra-Raspberry paint with a swoosh of his tail. (Sensing potential danger, she'd asked me to put the lid back on the paint ages ago. I promised her I would, then forgot 'cause I got distracted by watching *Extreme Animals* with Tor on CBBC.)

Anyway, Rolf ended up swooshing deep pink paint *all* the way down the left-hand side of the hall.

Luckily, Grandma is very thorough and efficient and managed to have it all scrubbed off by the time Dad and the rest of us (though not Linn) wrestled Rolf into the bath to scrub all traces of paint off his fur.

She's now gone home to her flat and is probably having a calming cup of peppermint tea in front of the Channel 4 news, and wondering if she made a big mistake offering to help us all out when Mum went off travelling. . .

Monday 8.03 p.m.

Wonder if I'll win any of the *Hornsey Journal* competitions? If I do, I'll give my prize to Grandma, for being lovely and making our tea and doing our laundry and always being here (except at weekends when she gets time off for good behaviour).

Though maybe she will be offended if it turns out to be the foot deodorizer. . .

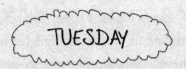

TUESDAY

Tuesday 7.45 a.m.

I'm a bit disappointed. I just undid the four plaits I slept in, and I look more like I have an unravelled brown woolly jumper draped across my head rather than glossy, rippling, crinkle-cut-chip waves like Libby-Mae Ferguson.

I think the problem is that I did the plaits different thicknesses. I should have concentrated more, but I put them in when I was thinking about what Erin's dad Dave said in the trade centre yesterday.

Well, he didn't say anything in *particular*; it was more the fact that he looked confused by what *I'd* said that properly confused me.

I'm being confusing, aren't I?

(Rule No. 8: *I will NOT be confusing.*)

But it was like this: while we queued to pay, Erin's dad Dave suddenly noticed my split lip.

"Been kick-boxing again, Rowan?" he joked. I like Erin's dad Dave. He jokes around a lot. And he likes me, 'cause I laugh when he jokes around, whereas Erin just groans and rolls her eyes.

"No, it's all Erin's fault," I joked back. "My brother hit me with a frisbee. It would never have happened if I'd met up with Erin yesterday afternoon like we were supposed to, instead of her having to go out shopping with you!"

That's when Erin's dad Dave looked confused.

Then, *kerching!*, it was our turn to pay, and the whole thing ended up forgotten.

And I was *so* excited about the idea of doing up my room that I forgot to ask Erin about it at school yesterday (though I *did* remember to get her to promise to help me paint this coming Saturday).

I will ask her about it today, for sure.

Though I'm concerned that excess fumes from the Ra-Ra-Raspberry paint and dog shampoo might have made some of my brain cells go woozy. I poured orange and mango fruit juice on to my bran flakes this morning and squeezed magnolia hand wash on to my toothbrush.

"WHAT'S THAT GOT TO DO WITH PAINT FUMES?!" said Linn. "WHAT'S YOUR EXCUSE FOR

BEING A DINGBAT THE *REST* OF THE TIME?!"

By the way, I have been thinking about Rule No. 5 (*I WILL do more things for my family*) and have decided that I'm NOT just going to sit back and let Dad and Linn cook tea at the weekends. *I'm going to cook too!*

I just have to figure out *how* to cook first...

Tuesday 10.32 a.m.

Well.

Or as detectives in olden-time dramas always say: well, well, *well.*

Mrs Wells (coincidence!) must have sensed that I am a new, improved, non-annoying version of me, even though I have only been that new, improved, non-annoying version of myself for sixty-three hours and fifty-five minutes now.

'Cause it turns out that she has nominated me for a community project that student teacher Miss Boyle is setting up!

I have to go to a meeting about it at lunch time in the library.

By the way, Ingrid and Yaz are here right now, sitting on the wall with me and Erin. Ingrid is trying to peek at this journal, I'm sure. I'm going to keep my hand around what I'm writing so she definitely can't see.

Oh, I have just noticed that I have Ra-Ra-Raspberry paint on my watch. Oops.

And my watch is saying that it's 6.46 p.m.

I guess I should have taken it off when I helped give Rolf a bath.

Tuesday 1.25 p.m.

Oooh, Miss Boyle is fantastic! You can tell she is a student teacher, 'cause she is standing talking in front of us just now, sounding all excited and enthusiastic and interested in her new project.

She also seems to think that we are pretty interesting too, whereas all the regular teachers think of us students as something dull and irritating that fills up their time between nice things like breakfast and the half-past-three home-time bell.

"Great to meet you!" she beamed at us all when we filed into the library ten minutes ago. She'd made out stickers with our names on, written in thick gold pen and with stars instead of dots over the "i"s. (She's my kind of girl. Even if William Smith from 9Y looked a bit confused by the mini constellation above his name.)

By the way, there are just four of us in Miss Boyle's group, all from my year. We are:

- William Smith, who is super-smart but likes to act crazy (he slapped his name sticker on his blazer upside down).
- Verity Simone Melly, who has beautiful long blonde hair, but tends to eat it. I think it's a stress thing. She talks a bit too much too, and I think both those nervous tics are due to the fact that her parents are obviously demented. I mean, how could they give a girl a name that can be shortened to Very S. Melly?
- Marlon Trueman, who seems pretty chilled-out and normal, though no one tends to mention to him the fact that we ALL know he got expelled from his last school for supergluing the head teacher's door shut, and. . .
- Me: Rowan Anastasia* Love.

Anyway, everyone's very excited by Miss Boyle's project, I can tell, 'cause she's just asked if we have any questions, and William, Marlon and Verity have all got their hands up. (Verity's even making that "Uh-uh!!" noise that little kids tend to do unconsciously when they're desperate to get picked.)

Well, everyone's got their hands up except me. I'm hoping Miss Boyle thinks I'm taking notes instead of just scribbling in my journal...

OK, about the project: I'm sure it will be very interesting. It's something about recycling in the community. Or *with* the community. (Or recycling the *community*, maybe?!) Most excitingly, it means we get out of the last two hours of school every Monday afternoon for the next three weeks. Yay!

And even *more* exciting than getting out of school and doing some kind of project with the very enthusiastic Miss Boyle is the fact that I have just decided – it's official! – that I have a Hero Crush on Libby-Mae Ferguson.

(Normal crush = you want to kiss someone. Hero Crush = you lust after someone's coolness and wish you could be a tiny bit as cool.)

She's sitting over in the corner on one of the library computers right now and I think I like *everything* about her.

I mean, even *before* this week – when Libby-Mae was just part of the floppy-fringe-and-hairband crew – I was quite intrigued by her, 'cause of her super-cute name, which sounded like the title of an old-time rock 'n' roll song or something (*"Hey, hey, hey, Libby-Mae!"*).

But now that she's gone all retro-hippy with her

long, auburn, crinkle-cut-chip hair, I can't stop checking her out. I've just spotted that she has on these patent-leather orange ballet pumps, even though we're only meant to wear black shoes at school, really. And when she turned round a second ago to get some chewing gum out of her bag (I think it was that strange cinnamon-flavour chewing gum . . . er, does that sound like too much of a stalker-y detail?), I saw that she was wearing a little sweep of black liner on her eyelids.

Oooh.

Gorgeous!

I don't ever think of wearing orange . . . I should try it! And I'm *definitely* going to get some black eyeliner, when I next get pocket money. Which is, like, *never*, since that £20 Dad gave me for paint was supposed to be a whole bunch of weeks' pocket money at once.

Hmm.

I still have £15 left over for room accessories.

Maybe I should buy lots of accessories *plus* eyeliner, so that I can look as interesting as my new room?

I wonder what accessories Libby-Mae Ferguson has in *her* room? Stuff that's very cool, I'll bet. Lots of art posters and interesting knick-knacks and great books and a *guitar* probably and a—

Uh-oh. Look away quick. Libby-Mae Ferguson has

just swivelled round in her chair and nearly caught me staring at her, which would've been *very* lame.

Will pretend I am now listening very intently to Miss Boyle.

I might actually find out a bit more about what her project actually *is*.

---

* Possible good middle name for me? Watched a programme about Princess Anastasia on TV last night; she was the seventeen-year-old daughter of the Russian czar, who was killed with her family during the Russian Revolution in 19-something-or-other. Bet she was regal and elegant and focused right to the end (yes, I have a Hero Crush on her too). I'm not about to be killed (hopefully), but think she might be a good role model for the new, improved, non-annoying me.

Tuesday 2.01 p.m.

Didn't find out any more about what Miss Boyle's project actually is.

Because of my brain condition, I hadn't noticed that the bell had gone — THAT was the reason Libby-Mae Ferguson had swivelled around and padded off out of the library in her patent-leather orange ballet pumps, along with everyone else.

As William and Verity and Marlon shuffled out, Miss Boyle twittered away, thanking us all like a very cute robin with excellent manners, and saying she'd see us back here on Friday at 1.30 sharp. Ooh, *more* skiving, apart from the regular Monday thing? Excellent!

Apparently, we are going to visit Alexandra Hill School (our school's rival!!).

Maybe we are going to recycle some of the students there. Ha!

But never mind that.

Check THIS out. It's some kind of flyer for a *fairy website*.

FIND YOUR
INNER FAIRY
AT
WWW.FIND-YOUR-INNER-FAIRY.COM

!!!

Libby-Mae Ferguson must have *dropped* it; it was on the carpet near the swivel chair she'd been swivelling on. I scooped it up when I was trailing everyone else out of the library.

Wow – so Libby-Mae's got an inner fairy and she's trying to find it!

She's even *more* interesting than I *thought*!!

If I was a normal person (i.e., had a computer in my house, and not a dad with no money and a phobia of technology), I would go online as soon as I got home and find out what it's all about.

I'll look it up on one of the library computers tomorrow lunch time. It's dog food curry on the menu on Wednesdays so I don't mind missing it.

Tuesday 9.50 p.m.

Realized that I messed up my rule about being more focused TWICE today.

First time: when Miss Boyle – who seems very nice and deserves to be listened to – was chattering on about her project and I wasn't *entirely* listening, and. . .

Second time: when Grandma was showing me how to cook spaghetti bolognese earlier (so I can take my turn cooking at the weekends). I was supposed to be writing down everything she was saying point-by-point, but when I read it back just now, it said. . .

- *Stir the mince in a frying pan till brown.*
- *Add two tablespoons of oil and a handful of*
- *Boil the*

I think there were just too many instructions and my

brain imploded. Also, there was someone on the radio talking about an old Johnny Depp film and I ended up doodling a drawing of Johnny with love hearts round him instead of writing bolognese instructions.

If you haven't guessed, I have a HUGE Hero Crush on Johnny Depp. Oh, and a normal crush too. (Erin says that's icky, because he is completely ancient. But do I care what she says*?!)

Anyway, I'm still going to tell Dad that I'll cook tea one night this weekend.

Though I may have to start small.

Maybe I'll just make everyone some sandwiches.

Or boiled eggs and soldiers.

* Yes, a little bit.

Wednesday 4.49 p.m.

"It looks weird."

That's what Erin said when she stared over my shoulder at the Find Your Inner Fairy website.

"It doesn't look weird, it looks *interesting*," I said back to her.

I was at Erin's house after school today, using her computer – and then we were going to watch a DVD of *The Princess Diaries*, which we've watched a trillion times, but who's counting?

(By the way, Erin's house is extremely normal compared with mine, with computers and DVDs and neutral colour schemes, etc., etc. I'm slightly jealous of the first two, but not of that last one; I love our mismatching colour scheme. Even if visitors sometimes find it a bit *ouch* on the eyes.)

Anyway, I was using Erin's computer 'cause all the

ones in the library were busy this lunch time, with people doing proper work on them, like looking up sites on recycling. People like Verity Melly, who'd obviously listened better than me to what Miss Boyle had to say yesterday lunch time.

I thought I should maybe ask Verity more about it, but decided not to, because she has this reputation for chattering *endlessly* once she gets started. And more importantly, I figured that admitting I wasn't listening properly to Miss Boyle might make me look very shallow and so I chickened out. (I was hovering and biting my nails so much as I *willed* people to hurry up and log out that Miss Whyte the librarian asked if I had an important assignment I needed to study for. I had to quickly hide the flyer so that she didn't spot all the glitter and fairy dust and think I was shallow too.)

"It's *way* weird. Read *that!*" insisted Erin, flicking her floppy brown fringe back far enough so that she could squint and frown at the computer screen.

The home page of the Find Your Inner Fairy website *did* surprise me a bit, I guess, mainly 'cause I was sort of expecting to see images of beautiful fluttery beings, like out of the old-fashioned illustrations that are hanging in our bathroom. (They're very pretty but wrinkly, since they were cut out of a Sunday magazine once by Mum and stuck in frames that have never exactly kept out the condensation.)

What I *hadn't* expected was a photo of quite a plumpish girl called Jacqui wearing huge ornate wings and a mini tutu.

!!!

But she looked great.

I mean, why *shouldn't* you dress like a mini-tutu'd fairy when you're quite plumpish?!

And she had this amazing make-up on: all rainbow hoops of eyeshadow and glitter-sprinkled cheeks.

Also, she seemed very smiley and happy, which made *me* feel very smiley and happy too. And definitely *not* weirded out. So what was Erin on about?

I read what she was pointing at, in case it was genuinely weird.

Underneath Jacqui's tutu (so to speak) it said:

The Find Your Inner Fairy Philosophy
We all have a fairy living inside us.
A fairy who is beautiful and brave, fun and funky,
    kind and kooky.
Are you ready to listen to your inner fairy and live
    a fluffier, more colourful life?

"Wow, that's *lovely*!" I told Erin.

Erin rolled her eyes at me the way she rolls them at her dad Dave when he tells jokes.

"What, thinking you've got something living inside you? That's *weird*," she said with a shudder. "I mean, seriously W-I-E-R-D!"

I wondered whether I should tell Erin that she'd spelt it wrong, but I didn't want to be mean.

Even if *she* was being a bit mean about the fairy website, and making a dreamy idea sound like having a bad case of worms.

But I guess that even though we're best friends, that's something I've never *got* about Erin; the whole weird-versus-interesting thing. (And it's not just Erin; *lots* of people are the same. *Most* people, actually.)

What I mean is, why is it *weird* – and not just quite *interesting* – that our cat Colin only has three legs? (Why is four better? Why is the sight of Colin and his minus-one-leg so freaky? Could he *help* it that he had a fight with a car and lost?!)

Or why is it *weird* – and not just quite *interesting* – to wear a top hat? (I found one at a jumble sale at school. Erin made me walk ten steps behind her when I wore it to the park one day. It was nice – I put a red ribbon round it and glued some fake geraniums to the front.)

Or *weird* – and not just quite *interesting* – that my mum is off backpacking around the world? (Whenever I mention it, I know people think I'm covering up the fact that she's in prison or a psychiatric unit or something.)

Or *weird* – and not just quite *interesting* – that my little brother Tor won't eat his food till he's made it into something first? (Erin practically frowned her face in half the first time she saw Tor make a mashed-potato yeti with peas for eyes and accompanying "AAARGHH"ing noises.)

Or *weird* – and not just quite *interesting* – to paint your nails blue? (Erin told me to keep my hands in my pocket when I arrived during a visit from her great-gran. I didn't realize that people who'd lived through the Second World War would be so disturbed by navy nail polish.)

Then I noticed something that definitely *was* weird.

"Where've all the squirrels gone?" I suddenly asked, spotting three empty shelves. "And where's Sir Timothy Nutkins?"

Erin pulled a face, scrunching all the freckles on her nose into a brown blob, as if I'd just insulted her.

"All the soft toys and ornaments, you mean?" said Erin. "They're *long* gone!"

They weren't all *that* long gone. The squirrels were all still there on the shelves and the bed when I was round last Thursday for tea.

"It's like, what if someone came round here and saw all that . . . *babyish* stuff?" Erin carried on, waving her arm vaguely around her lilac-walled room. "It *had* to go."

"Someone like who? *I* come round all the time, and it doesn't bother me!" I told her.

Considering that I live in a house that's painted loads of mad colours, is sort of falling down and is full of Mum-made art and an assortment of stray pets that Tor drags home, a few cute squirrel doodahs hardly stood out.

"Yeah . . . well . . . I dunno," said Erin, sounding all uncertain, like she'd confused herself. "I just mean people who matter, that's all."

???

Y'know, sometimes I wonder why me and Erin are best friends. But then Grandma says opposites attract, and different people can complement each other, and absence makes the heart grow fonder. (Er, don't think that last one quite fits here. But Grandma says a *lot* of wise things that I really appreciate but usually only half-understand.)

Before I could figure out what to say back, Erin's mum Gillian came knocking at the door with a tray of juice and shortbread biscuits.

"Ooh, I love your hair clips, Rowan!" she said, nodding at my sweetie-wrapper grips. "Did you make them? You're so imaginative! Isn't she, Erin?"

Erin just rolled her eyes at her mum, and went and flopped on the bed. She doesn't like it when her mum comes to her room, 'cause she thinks it's an invasion of her privacy. I kind of understand, but then I *really* like shortbread.

And I definitely like Gillian and the fact that she always has something nice to say about what I'm wearing or whatever.

I really appreciated it the time she told me that the ringlets I'd tried to put in my hair looked "luscious", when I'd spent the day being followed around by a bunch of Year Seven boys shouting "Baaaaaa!" at me.

Wednesday 9.18 p.m.
Have been lying very still on my bed (with Rolf) – trying to get my mind to stop tap-dancing off on to stupid subjects – so I could connect with my inner fairy.

But I failed due to Ally thumpering around her room upstairs to the Foo Fighters' *This Is A Call*.

Also, I'm pretty sure that Rolf ate leftover spaghetti bolognese tonight. It would figure, as he is allergic to tomatoes, and my room smells of silent but deadly farts.

(Bet Libby-Mae Ferguson doesn't have to put up with rock music pounding through her ceiling and dog indigestion.)

Wednesday 11.15 p.m.

Still awake. Still not found my inner fairy. Thinking about a ticket I saw on Erin's pinboard. It was for the new Pixar film. Think the date on it was Sunday's.

???

If Erin went to see it with her dad Dave instead of shopping with him, why didn't she tell me?

And why didn't I ask her?

Because I panic that I might annoy her, *that's* why.

Or maybe just *irritate* her, which is not quite so bad but almost. I think I irritate her quite a lot, and it's seriously *not* good to be an irritating friend.

Actually, I think I irritated her this afternoon by talking about Libby-Mae Ferguson and the Find Your Inner Fairy website and how humongously cool Libby-

Mae is. Best friends do not need to hear how humongously cool other girls are. Especially best friends who don't get the concept of Hero Crushes (Erin thinks they are most *definitely* "W-I-E-R-D" and not interesting).

Rule No. 9: *I will NOT be an irritating friend.*

THURSDAY

Thursday 8.45 a.m.

I'm on my way to school with Ally (sorry, my writing may go wibbly while I'm walking). This morning started badly, with me wafting, flappy-armed and fairy-style, down our garden path and along the pavement. But then I felt two pairs of Eyes Of Gloom on me . . . Mr and Mrs Misery-Guts from next door (ancient and moany Mr and Mrs Fitzpatrick). They really don't *get* "interesting". I think every time they see me, they wish there was a law against being different, *just* so they could call the police and report me for reckless weirdy-ness.

Thursday 3.46 p.m.

Ooooh, I did a bad thing.

I sort of . . . just *took* something, without giving it back.

Which technically means stealing, doesn't it?

My inner fairy would not be pleased. (If I'd found her, which I haven't.)

Anyway, here's what I did.

I was ~~noseying at~~ *observing* Libby-Mae Ferguson, who was sitting on the wall by the science block at morning break, with her legs crossed. She was swizzling a foot around, so that I could *just* about make out a white price sticker on the sole of her orange pump.

Quickly, I bent right over and pretended to tie my shoelace so I could see the sticker better and figure out which shop she got her mega-pumps from.

Then five things happened:

1) Libby-Mae Ferguson got up off the wall with her mates.
2) Libby-Mae Ferguson sort of stared at me (!!!!!!!), as if she had recognized a kindred spirit who was *also* searching for her inner fairy.
3) Watched Libby-Mae Ferguson walking away, and saw her fiddling with something on the lapel of her blazer, which then seemed to drop off without her noticing. Ran over and scooped it up – it was a tiny crystal fairy brooch, with a bent, sort of broken wing. So cute!
4) I realized that I was the only person left in the

playground (missed hearing the bell again). Decided I'd catch up with Libby-Mae Ferguson some time during the day and give her fairy brooch back to her. Good excuse to say hello.
5) Saw Libby-Mae Ferguson three times during the day, but didn't talk to her. Had Nervous Leg Syndrome and couldn't get my feet to walk in her direction.

Am at home with ill-gotten fairy with bent wing sitting on my bedside table. Oo-er.

New Rule (No. 10): *Thou shalt not steal.*

Actually, I think I just stole that rule from God – he already has copyright on that one.

Sorry, God.

Thursday 8.19 p.m.

Urgh. Maybe Libby-Mae Ferguson *wasn't* staring at me because she recognized a kindred spirit with an inner fairy too.

I think it was maybe because I was pretending to tie my shoelace and I was wearing flip-flops.

Couldn't see a shoe shop name on the sticker on the sole of her shoe, by the way, but did see "£24.99", which means I won't be buying myself a pair of orange patent-leather ballet pumps any time soon. . .

FRIDAY

Friday 4.33 p.m.

I'm sitting on the grass in the park at Alexandra Palace writing this.

There is a light breeze blowing, which is gently wafting my hair about.

I think I might look very interesting to anyone passing, like a young novelist, scribbling away.

What I'm *actually* scribbling might not be my novel (yet) but it *is* very interesting; I've just been to Alexandra Hill School, where me, William Smith, Verity Melly and Marlon Trueman all met our recycling "buddies"!

(That's one crucial thing I missed from the library talk the other day: the four of us from Palace Gates School have each been paired up with a Year Nine student from Alexandra Hill.)

William has been buddied with Omar, who is incredibly smiley.

Verity has been matched with an absolutely *tiny*, dainty girl called Bianca, whose wispy hair is as white as her name (in Spanish, that is). Together, they're like perfect blonde Barbie and Polly Pocket dolls or something. (*I* probably look more like a brown-haired Sindy that's been vandalized! Ha!)

Marlon's buddy is a handsome-ish Turkish boy called Yusuf, who was so lost in his *Maximum PC* magazine that it took three goes for Miss Boyle to introduce them to each other.

So who is my "buddy"? Only the *least* smiley boy in the universe. . . (Oh, dear.)

His name is Georgie. When I met him just now he was wearing his school uniform, football boots and a *very* grumpy expression.

"Hi!" I said, before we were made to shuffle into a seat and watch a short film on recycling.

Georgie just stuck his hands deeper in his trouser pocket.

"I'm Rowan," I babbled, anxiously noticing out of the corner of my eye that there was plenty of shy-but-friendly grinning and "All right?"ing going on between William, Verity and Marlon and *their* buddies.

Georgie didn't grin; Georgie didn't talk. The only thing Georgie did was ruffle his hand through his muddle of dark brown curls. I noticed he was kind of cute-looking, and had long, dark eyelashes; the sort that are *wasted* on a boy.

"But some people call me Ro for short," I babbled some more.

Georgie was doing a lot of scratching of his head. I hoped that it was down to nerves and not nits.

"And I guess yours is *long* for George?!" I babbled some more, just to fill the sticky silence between me and my new "buddy".

Despite the cute-looking face, at that second, he sort of looked at me like he wanted to kill me. Hmm, *that* was a good start.

"Short for *Georgina*," Georgie said in a grumpy-sounding but quite high voice.

And *that's* when I realized that my buddy boy was in fact a *girl*. . .

Friday 4.59 p.m.

I'm at home.

Had to suddenly stop what I was writing (above) due to a large Staffordshire Bull Terrier running directly towards me in Ally Pally park. Was scared it was going to eat me or this journal.

I love dogs (except Winslet when she is chewing on

something I'm fond of, like my feathery, light-up Tinkerbell pencil, RIP), but Staffies give me the heebie-jeebies because they seem to have an excessive amount of teeth for the size of their heads.

Luckily the Staffie stopped – about half-a-metre's eating distance away from me – when its owner shouted, "OI! DIESEL!! COME *BACK* HERE!" (There were actually *more* words used in that sentence, all of them too rude to repeat in this notebook.)

So I escaped, and came home to ponder.

Things I am pondering:

1) What to make for tea tomorrow night, now that Dad has said I can take a turn cooking.
2) If I should really have spent £4.99 of my £15 room accessories fund on a black liquid eyeliner from the chemist.
3) How to put black liquid eyeliner on. I've tried, and the black swoop above one eye looks gorgeous and elegant. The swoop on the other eye is more of a meander and makes me look like it was put on by a toddler wearing a boxing glove.

By the way, Ally vaguely knows Georgie – when I described her just now, she remembered her from a season of football games between our school and Alexandra Hill. She said all she could remember about her was that . . .

a) she was an ace football player;
b) she never talked,
c) she always wore an Arsenal football shirt when she wasn't in school uniform and . . .
d) her mum was famous for coming along to cheer on the games wearing lycra leggings while having the sort of bum you shouldn't really combine with leggings.

SATURDAY

Saturday 9 a.m.

It's PAINTING DAY!!!

Have been very <u>focused</u> (Rule No. 3; tick!) and planned it all out.

Here's how:

- I got up early and had a hearty breakfast for energy. (Three yoghurt cereal bars.)
- I got changed into my painting outfit. (Very pretty rose-patterned pyjamas that are sadly just about too small for me.)
- I moved a chair, a stack of magazines and my dressing table. (Will move heavy furniture like bed and wardrobe with Erin when she comes to help, which is any minute now.)
- I shooed all pets from the room in case of paint/fur mishaps. (Got hissed at by Colin, who'd curled up

and was happily shedding ginger fur on my school
uniform.)

- I got the paintbrushes laid out by the paint, ready to
go. (Dad said paint rollers would be easier, but when
I went out to the shed, one had green mould on it
and a slug seemed to be sleeping on the other one
and I didn't want to disturb it.)
- I am about to put this journal in a safe place (in
bathroom cupboard where spare toilet rolls are), so
it doesn't get Ra-Ra-Raspberried.

Wish me luck!!

Saturday 9 p.m.
Arrgh! Seriously miffed with Erin – she didn't show up
today. (Phoned her house and spoke to her mum Gillian,
who said she was in Despose. I didn't know where
Despose was, and thought it was maybe a part of
London where her dad Dave was doing a plumbing job.
That was until I mentioned it at tea time and Linn yelled,
"*INDISPOSED*, YOU MUPPET, RO! IT MEANS SHE'S
NOT AROUND!!")

But **yay!** I have finished painting my room, all by
myself!

But **arrgh** (again)! I had a slight problem with the

paint. . . Thing is, because my room is pretty big, with a bay window and everything, after I did about one and a half walls, I realized that I wasn't going to have enough to paint the rest!!! And 'cause it was an end-of-the-line colour, I'd *never* find another pot.

But **yay!** I had an excellent idea. 'Cause everyone was out and Erin didn't come, I hadn't been able to move the heavy furniture *anyway*, so I just painted AROUND it all!

Of course the problem is that I can never, *ever* move the furniture in my room, or I'll end up with wardrobe and bed-sized rectangles of daisy wallpaper showing, but that's OK.

But **arrgh!**, I was also painting round my big, framed poster of Johnny Depp in *Edward Scissorhands* and – oops – it fell off the wall. The glass broke, the poster got ripped, and it now looks like I have a *daisy* poster in the middle of the wall that my bed faces.

But **yay!**, Dad said I'd done really, really well, all on my own, and to celebrate, he was going to order a giant pizza for tea.

I was very, very pleased, because it was the night I'd promised to make tea for everyone, and . . .

a) I was too tired to do it, and

b) hadn't got a clue what to make.

Y'know, I think Dad probably guessed a) and b).

SUNDAY

Sunday 10.40 a.m.

Haven't won any competitions in the local paper yet, by
the way. But entered a whole load more just now, before
I turned this week's *Hornsey Journal* into my new room
accessories, i.e., newspaper flowers.

(Still have £10.01 of my room accessory fund. Not
sure what to spend it on. Probably not much.)

Competitions/giveaways entered this week:

- A sixty-piece cutlery set (chrome)
- A free shampoo and blow-dry on OAP day at Snipz
  Hair Salon, Wood Green
- Tube of Mosiguard mosquito spray plus two car-
  window sun shields
- A year's supply of Pampers Pull-Up trainer pants

Not a brilliant week for prizes, then, though Grandma

might like the shampoo and whatsit. Winslet and Rolf would be happy with the Pampers, I guess . . . tearing them to pieces would keep them amused for a bit.

CRAFT INSTRUCTIONS

Newspaper flowers

You'll need:
- 1 copy of the *Hornsey Journal* (or any newspaper!)
- Some wooden kebab skewers (for stems)

Instructions:
1) Cut some newspaper pages into roughly 20-centimetre squares, then fold one square over into a triangle, then fold into a triangle again, and again.
2) Get scissors (preferably NOT Linn's nail scissors or she'll flip out) and cut a wibbly-wobbly half-moon curve across the bit of the triangle with all the loose edges. Open up and go "Oooh, that looks all petal-y!"
3) Do loads of the above, and layer a few

together to make your flower.

4) Stick the "stem" through the middle of all the layers of petals. (Wrap a bunch of sticky tape around the end of the stick once you've stuck it through, and then do the same underneath to keep petals in place.)

5) Get caught using Linn's scissors and shouted at (if you're me).

Sunday 1.30 p.m.

Just been for a walk around Ally Pally with Dad and Ally and Tor and the dogs – Dad said I needed fresh air 'cause I'd slept in my Ra-Ra-Raspberry room all night but forgot to leave the windows and the door open like he'd told me to and I was suffering from poisoning by paint fumes this morning. (Headache, nausea, slightly delirious: mistook Tor's favourite toy, Mr Penguin, for one of the cats and got hysterical when I stood on him outside my bedroom door first thing.)

Anyway, our walk around Ally Pally was especially nice 'cause Linn didn't come. (She gave me SUCH a hard time for borrowing her nail scissors to make newspaper flowers this morning. She has now put a label on them saying "*Property of Linn Love*". The label is bigger than her nail scissors.)

While we were walking, we met up with Ally's best (boy) friend (not *boy*friend) Billy and his dog Precious.

Ally says Billy is a big muppet but she really likes him. He is very cute and goofy. Everyone *tries* to like his dog Precious but it's very hard, as he is a small, shivery and mean white poodle who goes "YAPPITY-YAPPITY-YAPPITY-YAPPITY-YAPPITY-YAPPITY-YAPPITY-YAPPITY-YAPPITY-YAP!" all the time.

Like today, Ally was trying to explain to him why I had raspberry streaks in my hair and on my left ear, and Billy couldn't make out a word of what she was saying for all the yappitting.

Then I couldn't make out what *he* was saying, except for the bit when he said, "Yeah, but what's going on with her *eyes*?"

I think I still need to have a steadier hand with the liquid eyeliner.

Sunday 7 p.m.

Did my first tea tonight for everyone!

Didn't go down very well.

"It's very important," I said, as I plonked bowls of soup in front of Dad and everyone, "to have *five* portions of fruit and vegetables every day. And this soup has exactly *five* portions in it!"

Tor already looked disappointed. Soup is his least favourite food, as it's very hard to make anything with it. (I'd thought of that and given him seven slices of bread-and-butter so he could model something on his side plate.)

"It's a funny colour. . ." said Ally, warily swooshing her spoon around in the bowl of light-browny-grey goodness.

"So . . . what kind of soup *is* it, Ro?" Dad said with an enthusiastic smile.

I tried to think of the three soup cans I'd opened and chucked together in the pot.

"Leek and potato . . . mushroom . . . tomato, oh, and—"

Before I got to say my special ingredient (the one I grabbed in a panic from the fruit bowl to make the portions up to five), I saw that Linn was prodding at a bouncing blob in her soup. She lifted it out with a spoon, stared at it, then began to growl. She was more scary than the Staffie in the park on Friday.

Uh-oh. I guess Rule No. 11 is: *I will NOT put raspberries in soup. . .*

Sunday 7.10 p.m.

For the last ten minutes, I have been lying on my bed,

trying to think fluffy, fairy thoughts.

But my thoughts haven't been very fluffy – my tummy's been rumbling too much. (May have to go and get an emergency sandwich. Only ate half my soup due to it being slightly disgusting.)

Unfluffy thoughts that I have had:

- How can I do a school project with a silent girl who hates me because I thought she was a boy?
- Will I have used up the whole of the liquid eyeliner tube before I ever learn how to put it on properly?
- Why didn't Erin come and help me yesterday and why hasn't she phoned back yet? (I'd text her if I had a mobile phone. Don't want to call her house *again* and speak to her mum Gillian, who is usually very nice to me, but started to sound kind of odd by the sixth time she picked up the phone this afternoon. She keeps just saying that Erin is out, and that she'll get her to ring me.)
- Have I badly irritated my best friend somehow?
- Will I ever find my inner fairy?
- And will I ever be as cool and intriguing as Libby-Mae Ferguson*?

Huh.

Y'know, I don't think I've *got* an inner fairy — more like a panic goblin. . .

Sunday 7.20 p.m.

I just realized that I'd sort of planned to do this journal week-by-week — like start on a Saturday every time — and have now overrun this first week by two days. Oops.

Will try to be more focused on that from now on and remember days of the week better.

And here is my last new rule of the week (and-a-bit). . .

Rule No. 12: *I will NOT eat emergency sandwiches over my journal while reading it through.*

(Wonder if Grandma will know how to get egg mayonnaise stains out of paper???)

Sunday 7.32 p.m.

Aaargh, aaarrgh, aargh!!

Tried to be helpful to my family (Rule No. 5)

and take the rubbish out just now.

But I had the tartan blanket from the sofa wrapped around my waist because I'd noticed I'd spilt mayonnaise on my school skirt too and stuck it quickly in the wash.

I'm not sure if I tripped over the bin bag or the blanket or Rolf or all three. But whatever, the bin went flying and the bag split open and the dog started barking. Mrs and Mrs Misery-Guts from next door scowled FIERCELY with their Eyes of Gloom at both me and all the mess.

And it was *extra*-terrible because the blanket had slipped down and I was wearing my Little Miss Chatterbox pants (aged nine) 'cause that was all I could find at the back of my drawer this morning.

Uh-oh.

I think I may be even MORE annoying and unimproved *now* than I was when I started this journal a week (and-a-bit) ago.

(Rule No. 13: *I will NEVER put rubbish out while only wearing out-of-date pants and a tartan blanket. . .*)

WEEK 2

MONDAY

Monday 7:45 a.m.

Feeling much fluffier today!

And there are three reasons for that...

1) Had an amazing dream in the middle of the night: I was a *huge* butterfly the size of a house, fluttering over a field full of neon-pink sheep. Excellent!

2) Woke up from butterfly dream by tripping over Rolf, and realized I'd sleepwalked to the living room, managing NOT to trip on any of our other pets on the way down the stairs. (Miracle.) Saw that Dad had fallen asleep on the sofa with the telly on, and get this – coincidence or what! – *there* on the screen was a whole bunch of butterflies fluttering around a field! OK, so it was an ad for Lenor fabric conditioner (dewy mountain gooseberry fragrance or something), but it really felt like it was some kind

of *message*. . . Maybe my inner fairy was trying to tell me to fly free; to be beautiful and brave and all that other inspiring stuff in the Fairy Philosophy on the Find Your Inner Fairy site. Or that I should ask Grandma to switch fabric conditioners, maybe? Whatever, it was fantastic, and I went back upstairs to sleep (after switching off the telly and chucking the tartan blanket over Dad) feeling like I was floating on air and not just slightly worn carpets.

3) Came downstairs this morning to find all the cats wearing macaroni necklaces that Tor had made for them. Awww!

Monday 7.47 a.m.

That big bare daisy patch on my Ra-Ra-Raspberry wall is really bugging me. Must find something new to put up there to replace Johnny Depp poster. Don't know what. Maybe a new Johnny Depp poster?

Monday 8.55 a.m.

Not feeling so fluffy.

I'm outside Mrs Wells' office, sitting on one of her padded chairs that make embarrassing squelchy noises if you try to move. I think the school deliberately bought squelchy chairs so that you don't get comfy and have to sit dead still and mull over what you've done wrong. (What *I've* done wrong is be caught wearing flip-flops to school. I did point out to the teaching assistant on playground duty that they were regulation black, but she *still* sent me to see Mrs Wells.)

William Smith is here too. He seems to have waxed the front of his hair into a cool *cone* shape. I like it.

I wonder what *he's* done wrong? Can't ask him, as he's got his iPod on very loud and doesn't seem to want to talk. I've just noticed he's pretending to sit on a seat but is *actually* just leaning his back against the wall and perching above clear air. It's slightly crazy, but maybe it's just his way of avoiding the squelchy-sounding chairs.

Monday 8.57 a.m.

Sorry, had to stop earlier, 'cause William Smith spoke to me!

He said, "So what are *you* seeing Mrs Wells for?" and I kicked up my feet and showed him my flip-flops.

"What's with those?" he asked, pointing to the red ribbons I'd tied on them. "They're nuts!"

He didn't say it in a *mean* way, though, so I just shrugged and smiled and took it as a compliment.

"What are *you* here to see Mrs Wells for?" I asked William.

"Ben Davidson called me a *mumble-mumble-mumble...*"

I didn't quite hear *all* of the last bit, but I got the fact that it was something extremely rude.

"So how come *you're* here instead of *Ben*?" I asked.

"I got caught throwing a library book at his head."

"Oh..." I muttered, slightly confused that a member of staff on playground duty was more stressed about a book-chucking incident than a nasty jibe at someone's expense.

"I missed and it broke the boys' toilet window. It was a hardback chemistry book," William explained, filling in the blanks in my understanding.

Ah ... OK.

Then I asked William what he was listening to on his iPod and he said Foo Fighters, and I said they were my sister Ally's favourite band!

I told him *my* favourite music was by Kate Bush (Mum's got all her old albums), and he said he'd never heard of her, and I said she sang sort of sweet and dreamy and slightly mad songs and he said that sounded very bad but sort of *figured*.

!!!

Then we spoke about our recycling "buddies" from Alexandra Hill School.

William said his buddy Omar is Somalian and doesn't speak much English (which is why he just smiled a lot yesterday), but they'd bonded over the fact that they both had Manchester United school bags.

Then he laughed so much when I told him about me thinking Georgie was a boy that he didn't hear Mrs Wells calling him in.

By the way, I am *definitely* going to be brave today (Rule No. 14). This is hard because I'm not a very brave person. Actually, Linn says I'm like a jelly inside, but that's usually 'cause I've gone wobbly because of her getting all annoyed and shouting at me about something or other. Again.

Still, the new, improved, non-annoying me WILL be brave, and so I'm going to. . .

1) ask Erin *straight* out what's going on with her;
2) walk *straight* up to Libby-Mae Ferguson and give her back her broken-wing fairy brooch, and . . .
3) apologize *straight* away to Georgie when I see her later, and tell her I'm very sorry for thinking she was a boy, though it's not my fault because she dresses a lot like one. (Or something more tactful.)

May have to do deep-breathing exercises to curb my panic goblin before I do any of those.

Monday 10.15 a.m.

I have my journal open on my lap. (It's now covered in gingham fabric and fancy buttons and a bunch of juicy raspberry stickers. My journal, I mean – not my lap.)

I'm writing this in a cubicle of the temporary loos on the first floor, while the normal girls' loos are out of action. They are very nice toilets, because they are the Female Visitors' Toilets, and have fancy hand wash and fake flower displays. Oh, and no graffiti. Yet.

Anyway, everything is OK with me and Erin. Phew! After Mrs Wells let me go back to class (she gave me a not-very-stern warning about flip-flops being illegal at school or something), I sat down next to Erin in class and she apologized and explained why she couldn't come on Saturday and why she didn't get in touch.

Well, sort of.

What she *actually* said was, "Yeah, sorry about the weekend. I had a cold", while not really looking at me.

That's all right, though, isn't it?

I'm pretty sure it is. (Though not quite sure why her mum Gillian didn't just say so.)

And Erin offered me a Polo at the same time, so that *proves* everything's normal.

She also reminded me that it's *this* Sunday that her dad Dave and mum Gillian are taking us to the circus in Alexandra Palace – just like they've done for the last couple of years. Excellent!

So . . . since I didn't have to use any of my braveness on Erin, it means I have *extra* for whenever I bump into Libby-Mae Ferguson, AND when I have to meet Georgie-who's-NOT-a-boy later.

Ooh. . .

I can hear squeak-squeak-squeaking and some sniggering going on in the next cubicle.

That is either the sound of very giggly mice, or a couple of someones writing something they shouldn't with a marker pen.

(Don't think it's mice.)

CRAFT INSTRUCTIONS

Cute book cover
You'll need:
- Some delicious material
- A few buttons or beads

- Stickers
- Fabric glue

Instructions:
1) Choose the book you want to cover (maybe a journal, or a very wordy science book you want to make look more friendly).
2) Cut out a piece of cloth a few centimetres bigger than the book.
3) Neatly fold the material into the inside of the front and back cover (a bit like you're gift-wrapping it), and glue the folds in place (beware of getting glue on the pages, like I did on my favourite book, *When Hitler Stole Pink Rabbit* by Judith Kerr. Now I have a gorgeous copy covered in pink fluffy material, but I don't know what happens between pages 56-89).
4) Glue on pretty buttons and stick on stickers to decorate.

Monday 12.30 p.m.

I've had no bumping-into moments (bumpage?) with Libby-Mae Ferguson, so her wonky-winged fairy will have to stay in my pocket for another day.

Which means, of course, that I can use all my braveness to face Georgie-who's-NOT-a-boy! (On our way to Alexandra Hill School now. Wish myself luck. . .)

Monday 2.38 p.m.

I have just seen the most AMAZING thing. It's like my *dream* home!!

Well, if I was old enough to *have* my own home, and didn't mind that it was a Portakabin at a rubbish dump. . .

Where am I? Well, right now I am sitting in a (different) darkened Portakabin in our local Reuse and Recycle Centre (i.e., dump). An education officer from the borough is showing a film about pollution and landfill around the world on a whiteboard.

It's very interesting (I think), but I am more excited about what I've just seen and I want to write it down quickly in case it boings out of my mind when I'm not looking.

(It's OK; I can still manage to write because there's enough light from the film and I'm using a luminous pink glitter gel pen.)

Here's the thing: I had never been to our local Reuse and Recycle Centre before and thought it would be dull, dull, dull, but it's not, not, *not!*

First we got to clamber up all these steps and look

into *giant* skips that were full of different things that people chuck away, like clothes and fridges and old mattresses and toys and stuff, which all get recycled, though I'm not sure how, but that's what the education officer told us when she was showing us round.

(That's not the amazing thing, by the way.)

Next, the education officer pointed out all these brilliant mosaics around the walls of the centre, which were about recycling (duh!) and were done by local schools, including Alexandra Hill School, according to Bianca, Verity's doll-size buddy.

(That's not the amazing thing either, if you hadn't guessed.)

Finally, the education officer pointed to the dump office. I hadn't noticed it before, thanks to a van being parked in the way. But right then, as if by magic, the van rolled off, and revealed the AMAZING sight!

The whole front of the Portakabin was *covered* in found things; stuff that people had come to chuck in the giant skips, but had been rescued by the staff.

It was like Hansel and Gretel's Gingerbread House, only with random fabric flowers, plastic bath ducks, loops of fairy lights and drapes of Christmas decorations instead of sweets.

Cracked terracotta pots had faded children's

windmills on sticks planted in them, fluttering and whirring in the breeze.

Slightly wonky mismatching mobiles were swirling and tinkling from the guttering.

A row of once-loved soft toys and dolls sat on a rusty wrought-iron bench under the window.

Honestly, all I'd need to do was paint the inside Ra-Ra-Raspberry and I'd move in tomorrow!

Actually . . . now I think about it, the office looks like a mini-version of *our* house, only more mental. Excellent!

Ooh—

The education officer has put the film on pause *right* at a bit where some poor kids in India are scrabbling round a really revolting tip for stuff they can find to sell so they can eat.

She must be about to ask questions.

I better pay attention.

Monday 2.42 p.m.

Oops. The education officer wasn't asking questions just now — she wanted to find out what the annoying slap-slap-slapping sound was.

Georgie pointed to *me*.

It was apparently my flip-flop flap-flap-flapping on

the floor in my excitement, and I didn't realize.

P.S. I haven't managed to say anything to Georgie except "hello" so far this afternoon. And so far, she hasn't said anything – including "hello" back – either. But it's not the end of our session yet, and I WILL be brave and talk to her properly. Cross my heart and hope to etc., etc.

Monday 4.43 p.m.

Wow, wow, wow!!! Before we left the Reuse and Recycle Centre, a guy who worked there – well, he was wearing a high-visibility yellow vest so he was either working there or a bit strange – saw me drooling one last time at their cutely nuts office building/the inspiration for my future home.

And guess what he gave me? A box full of *fairy lights*! One multicoloured, one flowery and one with pink fluffy bits FOR *FREE*.

!!!

I have just strung them all around my room, and even before I've put them on, I know they are going to look WOW!!!

But I'm going to be very patient and not switch them on yet. Oh, no. I haven't even shown them to Grandma or Linn or Ally or Tor. That's because I'm going to wait till Dad gets home, invite everyone up here, and have a ceremonial turning-on of the lights, just like celebs do for the Christmas lights in Regent Street!

I'm so excited, I'm going to have to dress up. I may even try to put my liquid eyeliner on.

Monday 4.59 p.m.

Plan ruined, liquid mascara halfway down my face due to crying.

Linn spoiled *everything*!

She was coming down the stairs from her attic bedroom when she saw me going into my room dressed in Mum's vintage '70s halter-neck maxi dress with a tray of Jammie Dodger biscuits and wondered what was going on.

So she FOLLOWED me, DEMANDED to know what I was up to, FLIPPED OUT when I told her about my second-hand lights, and then CONFISCATED them due to health and safety regulations or something.

???

Then Grandma came up when she heard all the kerfuffle, and I *tried* to get her to stop Linn unplugging my lights but she said she had to agree with Linn, and that second-hand electrical things had a habit of blowing up and burning houses down, which seemed like a *bit* of an exaggeration.

Waiting till Dad comes home now, to see what *he* says.

Staying in my room and not speaking to anyone.

Except Rolf and Winslet, who have hung around to share the Jammie Dodgers with me.

And Ally, who gave me up a strawberry Frube yoghurt tube just now to cheer me up.

And Tor, who brought in his latest stray pet to give me a cuddle (it's a very, very big garden snail).

TUESDAY

Tuesday 12.20 p.m.

Felt too unfluffy to write again last night.

Dad said no to the fairy lights till he checked them out. (It turns out that Grandma *wasn't* exaggerating; houses *have* burned down due to dodgy fairy lights. Eeek!)

Anyway, I don't know quite *how* Dad is planning on checking them out exactly (maybe test them at his shop? String them all over the bicycles he's repairing?), but I don't hold out much hope.

But, y'know, I'm pretty much OK today.

Wolfed lunch (tortillas in the dining hall – mmm!) and I'm now sitting in the library, waiting for a computer to become available.

I decided that to act more like the new, improved, non-annoying me (i.e., Rule No. 1), I should start researching recycling ideas. That's 'cause Miss Boyle explained to us yesterday that we're NOT just getting together with the Alexandra Hill students to *learn* about recycling. Nope, we are meant work *together* with our buddies and come up with excellent ideas to <u>Raise Awareness of Recycling in the Community</u>.

This is because there's going to be a *big* exhibition about the environment and recycling happening in Crouch End Town Hall Square on a Saturday in just a couple of weeks' time. Miss Boyle says the mayor will be there (ooh!) and so will the local newspapers (double ooh!!), and she wants us to have a stall or something and be able to show-and-tell the mayor and the papers all our excellent ideas.

!!!

I REALLY WANT TO DO THIS, AND DO IT *WELL*!! Not *just* because of the environment, but because it will show everyone once and for all that I am so OVER being annoying, and that I am *definitely* a New and Improved, Non-Annoying Me and Full of Focus (Rules 1 and 3).

So I need some *fast*. Excellent ideas, I mean.

Of course, it would help if me and my buddy were actually *talking*, but there was so much going on at the Reuse and Recycle Centre yesterday that I didn't have time to apologize to Georgie-who-is-NOT-a-boy.

OK . . . so *technically*, I failed Rule No. 14 (being

brave), but that's because I spotted Georgie looking at me up and down like I might be toxic when we were next to each other by the Green Waste skip.

I mean, I was in my school *uniform*, so what was the big deal?! The only things that were mildly unusual were my ribbon-y flip-flops.

Oh, and yeah, so I had my hair in two plaits with leftover red ribbon braided into it.

And I was wearing a macaroni necklace that Tor made me, after he'd finished doing them for the cats and dogs this morning.

But, y'know, so *what*?!

EEEEEEKKKK!

Libby-Mae Ferguson and her crinkle-cut-chip hair and patent-leather orange ballet pumps has just walked into the library!

She is going over to the low-down seats by the non-fiction section, with a couple of her mates.

Gulp.

Her fairy brooch is in my pocket; I should just march over and give it to her right now. I could say, "Hi, Libby-Mae! I think this is yours!", and she will take one look at me and my not-so-crinkly hair (one plait came out and unravelled in the night, so I have crinkly waves on one side and straight floppiness on the other), and think I am maybe worthy of talking to, even if I am only Year Nine. Maybe I'll mention the Find Your Inner Fairy website too, so she realizes we have lots in common.

OK, I am going to be brave, I *really* am.

I'm going to take a few deep breaths, then I'm going to put this journal away, get up and walk ri—

Oooooh!

I've just noticed she's wearing sparkly green eyeshadow!!

That is *sooooooooo* gorgeous!

She's all cascading hair and iridescent eyes, with this ethereal aura, like a heroine in a Pre-Raphaelite painting* (only wearing school uniform and shiny patent-leather shoes).

Can't possibly speak to her now.

She's WAY too amazing.

---

* Like the painting I saw on a school trip to the Tate Britain, *Ophelia* by Sir John Everett Millais . . . it's just *gorgeous*, with the tragic heroine floating serenely in the water with her hair spread out and flowers drifting around her. Sadly, Ophelia *is* a bit dead in it. (Rowan Ophelia Love. . .?)

Tuesday 6 p.m.

Just noticed that I used a lot of great words towards the end of my last entry. Quite impressed with myself.

Think Rule No. 15 should be: *I will try to have a MORE varied and cultured vocabulary.*

Brill.

Anyway, bought glittery lemon eyeshadow from the chemist's on the way home today (only colour they had). Nice! Though I now have only £7.02 for room accessories. Don't think I can get a giant mirrorball with that. Maybe one small mirror *tile*. . .

Had a really cool time with Erin after school, by the way. She came back and we watched *Pretty In Pink* together. It's a very old video of my mum's. At our house, we've got lots of old films on video (not DVD) and a very temperamental old player that spits videos out if it's not in the mood to play them.

But it behaved for us today, so we took over the living room and slobbed. With cookies.

That's the thing: me and Erin may have different tastes in clothes, hairstyles, bands, boys, what's-weird-versus-what's-quite-interesting, Hero Crushes, find your inner fairy websites and just about EVERYTHING else, but *wow* do we both like watching movies — *any* kind of movie. Her favourite ever is *The Fifth Element* (futuristic fantasy starring edgy actress Milla Jovovich) and mine is *The Sound Of Music* (corny old musical starring singing kids and nuns).

Well, it was all going fine till we paused the film for a juice break and then Erin squinted at me and my glittery yellow eyeshadow.

"Do you like it?" I asked her, fluttering my eyelashes for fun.

"Well. . ." Erin said slowly, picking her words. "It sort of makes you look like you've got some weird *skin* disease."

She didn't pick her words very well.

"What made you choose that colour, anyway?" she asked, helping herself to some tropical squash.

I stopped myself from mentioning Libby-Mae Ferguson's gorgeous, sparkly (green) eyelids, in case that bugged Erin.

So I changed the subject and told her about William Smith finding a kid's broken toy tank at the dump yesterday, and how Marlon Trueman snapped a couple of rocket launchers off it and taped them to the back of William's school blazer so it looked like he'd got turbo boosters. William took off around the recycling centre car park till one of the staff shouted that the car park was for vehicles only, and William pointed at his turbo boosters and said, "But I'm the Millennium Falcon! That's a vehicle, isn't it?!"

It was a completely stupid thing to say, but pretty

funny to watch him (we'd *all* thought it was pretty funny – I even saw Georgie almost smile), but Erin didn't seem to get it.

"Huh?"

So I changed the subject (again) and asked what she wants to do for her birthday instead.

"Dunno," she said, which seemed pretty lame, since it's only about a week and a half away. Last year we had it planned for *months*; Erin's mum Gillian took us to the West End and we shopped for days (it felt like) in the ginormous Topshop at Oxford Circus, then went to Pizza Express and ate *way* too much, and then we went to the IMAX and saw a special screening of *Harry Potter* (can't remember which one) in 3D. It was excellent!

"But you've got to do *something* good for your fourteenth birthday!" I said.

"Not bothered," Erin shrugged, looking in the mirror on the kitchen wall and smoothing her floppy fringe to the side.

I thought maybe she was stuck for ideas, since last year had been so much fun. So I suggested a couple of low-key things.

"We could go hang out at Camden Market and look at the weirdy-beardy stalls and get a henna tattoo?!"

"Nah."

"How about London Aquarium – you can stroke the stingrays if the attendants aren't looking!"

But Erin just did that thing where her nose crinkles up and her freckles merge disapprovingly. So I went back to hunting for snacks in the fridge.

"Actually, *Ingrid* said something that sounded kind of interesting. . ." she suddenly muttered.

"Oh, yeah?"

"Yeah. She said for *her* birthday a few months ago she went ice-skating up at the Alexandra Palace rink with Yaz and a few mates, and then went for a burger afterwards."

"Sounds good!!" I said, immediately wondering what sort of skating outfit I could come up with. Something with a cute frilly skirt. . . And *sequins*! There're always *gazillions* of sequins spangling away on those ice-skating shows on TV.

Anyway, that seems to be me and Erin's outing for her birthday sorted, I think.

But, y'know, I'm actually starting to panic about what I'm going to get her for a present. I don't think I can give her the squirrel knickers any more, since she's not into Sir Timothy Nutkins and his mates these days, AND because she's been shamed about them in front of wise-guy boys like Ben Davidson and his mates. (Ben's fault; not mine.)

There is probably a whole world of wonderful things out there I could get her, but as I have a budget of £7.02 (room accessory funds), it's not looking too promising.

If only life was simple (and still squirrelly)...

Tuesday 7.34 p.m.
Wheeee!!

Dad saved his pretty EXCELLENT news till after tea.

Get this: on the way to work this morning, he cycled past the Reuse and Recycle Centre, and went and SPOKE to the nice man in the yellow fluoro safety vest! Yeah, the one who gave me the box of fairy lights!! And it turns out he is a *trained* electrician who thoroughly checked and approved all the lights.

!!!

Apparently, the recycling guy *did* tell me that at the time, but I think I was too overawed by the pink fluff and reams of tiny, sparkly bulbs to pay attention properly.

So they are all BACK UP and **ON**!!!

My room is looking fantastic, and will look even

MORE fantastic once I figure out what room accessories to buy with my remaining vats of money. Ho, ho, ho.

Oh! Except I have a birthday present to buy with them.

Sigh.

Tuesday 10.06 p.m.

Tor was a bit upset at bedtime. Graham, his newest pet (the really, really big garden snail), has slithered off from the shoebox Tor was keeping him in and escaped somewhere.

("Do you think Winslet's eaten it?" Ally whispered to me, while we helped Tor and Dad search the house. Winslet eats a lot of things she shouldn't – hair clips, bus passes, tubes of toothpaste – but she's more of a magpie, into stuff she thinks in her doggy brain is treasure. I think snails would be below her. Hopefully.)

Anyway, we didn't find Graham. And to make up for it, we ALL took a turn reading Tor a bedtime story. My turn came last, and it gave me a *great* idea. (Not the book I was reading, by the way, because it was about pirates. Pirate *cats*. Tor doesn't do stories about people.)

So I read Tor the story, and afterwards, he wanted me to stroke his head like a dog and tell him something interesting till he got sleepy.

The first thing that popped into my head was the Find Your Inner Fairy website, since I checked out *that* at lunch time, instead of looking up useful recycling sites for my project. (Oops!)

Was EXTREMELY excited when I realized there's a whole online store section in there, where you can buy stuff like tutus and wands and sparkly bubbly bath and the most BEAUTIFUL hand-painted fairy wings, for a very reasonable squillion pounds. (Pah.)

I explained to Tor about how "Jacqui", who runs it, says that everyone has an inner fairy who will help them be brave and beautiful and all the other nice stuff.

He said he thought that sounded *ace*, and how he'd love to have an inner penguin, who would help him find a way to get to the Antarctic and introduce him to polar bears.

He was getting a bit too excited by that time, so I had to switch tactic and tell him some recycling facts ("Did you know that the largest lake in Britain could be filled with rubbish from the UK in eight months?", "Did you know that plastic can take up to five hundred years to decompose?"). *That* soon had him snoozling off.

And while I waited for him to fall asleep, I found

myself watching his gerbil (Thor), who was busy scuffling around among the little bits of shredded Sunday newspaper lining its cage.

That's when I had my idea . . . if I was having problems finding my inner fairy, maybe I could *make* her!

Thank goodness I never, *ever* throw out copies of old magazines!!!

CRAFT INSTRUCTIONS

(Patchwork) inner fairy

You'll need:
- Tiny, ripped-up squares of magazine, all sorted into different colours
- Glue
- Glitter

Instructions:
1) Draw your fairy on a bit of card.
2) Glue the tiny ripped-up squares of magazines collage-style in appropriate places (mine has a lilac dress and wings that merge from blue to green to yellow, and red hair; a

bit like Libby-Mae Ferguson's).

3) Cut out extra details from magazine, e.g.,
   model's face and hands, to personalize your
   fairy; pictures of small flowers to add
   texture to dress, etc. Glue on, then sprinkle
   glitter where you want.

4) Cut out your inner fairy and stick her in a
   secret, special place, where you can whisper
   to her when you're in need of fluffiness. . .

WEDNESDAY

Wednesday 10.03 a.m.

Sitting in a cubicle in the Female Visitors' Toilets.

Wasn't feeling very fluffy this morning, so came in here to have a chat with my inner fairy (now glued into the back of this journal).

Not feeling very fluffy because when I came into school this morning, I saw Erin standing laughing her head off with Ingrid and Yaz. (That's OK – laughing is allowed.)

I started smiling in advance, hoping to join in with the laughing, but when I got closer and they noticed me, Ingrid and Yaz stopped. Laughing, I mean.

"Hi, guys!" I said, trying to sound cheerful. "What's up?"

Ingrid and Yaz didn't say anything; they just flicked their long fringes out of their eyes and stared at me.

"Oh, nothing much!" said Erin, flicking her long fringe out of *her* eyes.

Which immediately made me think it WAS something much.

Feeling a bit wibbly inside, I tried to change the subject and said, "So what are you going to wear to the circus on Sunday, Erin?", because I had already planned my outfit (stripy tights, denim shorts, hippy smock top of Mum's, beanie hat that I'd sewn luminous beads on to).

Ingrid and Yaz sort of *laughed*, but I don't know whether they thought my *question* was stupid or going to the *circus* was stupid.

Erin went a bit red and looked annoyed with them (I think) and said, "Gawd! I dunno, *do* I?"

Then the bell rang.

In our first class, I whispered to Erin and asked her why Ingrid and Yaz had gone all weird (and not interesting) on me and she said it was probably because of my yellow sparkly eyeshadow. She said they maybe thought I had conjunctivitis.

Can't remember what conjunctivitis is meant to be, but know it's not a compliment. Didn't ask Erin why she'd seemed annoyed becau—

Oh!

Think someone's crying in the next cubicle!

Wednesday 10.11 a.m.

I'm back.

The person crying in the next cubicle was Verity Melly.

"What's wrong?" I asked her, once on the outside of her cubicle and once on the *inside* when she flipped the bolt and let me in.

Verity was crying too much to talk (unusual for her). Instead she just pointed at some graffiti on the back of her cubicle door. At first I thought she meant the scrawl about Mr Grayson the art teacher being a "*total hunk 4 sure!!*" (true, and nothing to cry about).

But that wasn't it.

Just underneath was this: "*Q: What's wrong with class 9E? A: There's a Very S. Melly girl in it!*"

Poor Verity. I tried to cheer her up by telling her she could legally get married and change her name (in Scotland) in only three years, but she just kept snivelling.

Then my mouth came up with a joke that was in bad taste and started saying it before my brain could tell it to shut up. (Nooooo!)

"Though knowing *your* luck, you'll fall in love with someone called Mr *Tupid*. . ."

Luckily, Verity doesn't seem to have the same dumb

sense of humour as me and didn't get it.

"Huh?"

"Nothing," I said, grabbing some loo roll for her to blow her nose on.

While Verity trumpeted, I tried to cheer her up by telling her that everyone thought I had conjunctivitis because of my eyeshadow.

Good; she managed a snotty snigger to that.

Actually, she seemed a smidgen more composed (note: good use of vocabulary, i.e., Rule No. 15 – big tick!) by the time she left the loos a minute ago. I could tell because she'd started to talk too much. ("Thank you. I think I'm OK now. I'll go and find my friends. What time is it? They were downstairs by the water fountain, but if it's nearly bell time they might have already gone to the language block 'cause it's French next. But then they *might* still be waiting for me" etc., etc.)

So yep, she was a lot less stressed-out than when I found her.

Still, I think there will be a *lot* of hair eaten today. . .

P.S. There's a whole load of glitter on the floor of the loos, by the way. Think my inner fairy is shedding.

Wednesday 5.09 p.m.

What a busy time I've had since school!

It has involved unexpected bargains and bicycle spray paint.

Here's what happened: I thought I should go to Wood Green Shopping City after school, to look for potential Erin presents. (Maybe a lie detector, so I could figure out what was going on with her and Ingrid and Yaz when they "weren't talking about 'anything'".)

Couldn't find any good presents (especially for £7.02). And then I accidentally went into this shop having a closing-down sale and bought a PAIR OF BALLET PUMPS FOR ONLY £2.50!!!

They are EXACTLY like Libby-Mae Ferguson's, except for the fact that they are made of canvas and not shiny patent leather, and they are a sort of yucky mushroom colour and not orange.

But straight away I knew a way I could fix that!

So I got on the bus and headed for Dad's shop . . . and borrowed a tin of orange bicycle spray paint from him! After tea, I'm going to spray my bargain shoes so they look *just* like Libby-Mae Ferguson's.

That way it'll be great at school tomorrow – me and Libby-Mae will have something in common, and she'll smile at me 'cause we are kindred spirits (good vocabulary; tick!). And *then* I will present her with her long-lost fairy brooch, which she'll be *extremely* grateful for; and she'll take me under her wing and imbue me with her effortless coolness and we can chat about inner fairies. Maybe she'll even show me how to put on liquid eyeliner straight.

Actually, I've just had an excellent idea! Maybe I could go back and buy *another* pair (still have £4.52, after all) and spray some shoes for Erin's birthday! *Great* thinking. . .

Wednesday 7.30 p.m.

Aargh!!!

What have I done!!!

I just held my shoes up to spray them orange, but realized too late that I should have done it outside or at least put newspaper down on the floor. There's now a fine spray of orange paint on part of my bedroom carpet.

Eeek!

Wednesday 7.33 p.m.

Had a word with my inner fairy. She suggested I send a fine spray over the *rest* of the carpet, so it gives a nice overall, uniform effect.

Think it looks OK. Sort of.

Need a wee, but can't leave the room till the paint dries. (Says six to eight hours on the can. Uh-oh.)

By the way, I think I know where Graham the missing garden snail is, roughly. There are wiggly, silvery trails going up and down the wall where the ex-Johnny Depp daisy rectangle is.

I will search for Tor's tiny friend in the morning, when the paint on the carpet is dry.

THURSDAY

Thursday 7.19 a.m.
WINSLET HAS EATEN MY NEW EYESHADOW!!
(RIP.)

Sigh. . .

I thought that waking up with a headache this morning from paint fumes (again) was bad enough.

But then I got out of bed a few minutes ago – half-asleep – and went to the loo. On the way back, I glanced down and saw I'd walked glittery yellow footprints all across the carpet. They went quite well with orange mist of paint (I think) but I was still a bit discombobulated by the sight of it nevertheless (good vocabulary; tick!).

Then I heard the crunching of plastic coming from under the bed. That's when I got down on my knees and spied Winslet under the bed crunching her latest treasure, i.e., my eyeshadow palette.

115

And *now* Rolf has just come in the room and started licking the glittery carpet and *sneezing*. . .

Still, maybe it's for the best; I looked up conjunctivitis in our Family Health Encyclopaedia last night and it didn't sound very gorgeous.

Thursday 7.24 a.m.

Omigod, omigod, omigod!!

The postman delivered a squashy parcel addressed to ME just now. And it's *only* the six free packets of Wall's sausages!!!

YEP, I WENT AND WON A COMPETITION IN THE NEWSPAPER!

It's the start of me being more useful to my family! Maybe I can make a stew with the sausages for tea one night! (Wonder how you do that?)

Oh, it's a fantastic sign.

I'm going to have an EXCELLENT day!!!

Thursday 10.03 a.m.

Not having an excellent day so far.

Reasons being. . .

- When Tor came into my room to look for Graham the snail earlier this morning, Linn was behind him and saw my carpet, and said, "WHAT HAVE YOU *DONE*, YOU DINGBAT?!"

- Linn called Dad and Grandma upstairs to see my stupidness for themselves, and the sense of annoyance in the air was palpable (good vocabulary; tick!). Though Dad did seem to veer between sighing and looking like he might snigger, just like he did when I went into his shop yesterday and told him my ballet-pump-and-paint plans.

- Tor couldn't find Graham and went into meltdown when Grandma said they had to get going or they'd be late. (As Tor howled, Grandma flashed me a "Couldn't-you-have-told-him-*after*-school?" glance that was full of palpable annoyance. Again.)

- Mr and Mrs Misery-Guts from next door were out in their garden when I went zooming off to school, and both started tutting and shaking their heads at my orange pumps.

- When I walked into the playground, Erin looked at my shoes, scrunched the freckles on her nose together, and didn't say anything. (Guess a customized pair of pumps might not be her dream birthday present, then?)

- Bumped into Marlon Trueman right after that, who grunted at me and asked how I was getting along with my recycling project. Apparently, he and his recycling buddy Yusuf (the Turkish boy from Alexandra Hill) have been emailing ideas to each other, and Verity and Bianca are texting each other non-stop. Help! I'm not even *speaking* to Georgie-who-is-NOT-a-boy!! William and Omar have probably already invented a solar-powered wind turbine made entirely out of Yakult pots.

- The orange paint on my shoes has started to flake off.
- I'm staring right this second at the back of the cubicle door in the Female Visitors' Toilets, reading a bit of graffiti that isn't about Mr Grayson the hunky art teacher or Verity (S.) Melly this time. Instead, it says, "*Rowan Love is a total freak!*" I don't think it's meant in a friendly way.
- Started to feel a little sorry for myself and snivel a bit, so put my hand in my pocket for a tissue – and pricked my finger really badly on Libby-Mae's fairy brooch.
- It won't stop bleeding.

Have just had a word with the inner fairy at the back of this journal, and she suggested I stay in this cubicle and never, ever leave. . .

Thursday 10:45 a.m.

Miss Boyle has just click-clacked off on her kitten heels to raid the staffroom first aid kit for a plaster. (She noticed I was getting blood on my choc-chip cookie – bleurgh.)

I should really be in French just now, but instead, I'm drinking tea and eating cookies (and bleeding) with Miss Boyle, who is extra-specially lovely, I've decided.

I'm here thanks to Verity Melly. She may not understand my sense of humour, and I may not share her taste for hair, but at least we can rely on each other in times of grafitti.

She'd been the last person in the toilets when the end-of-break bell went, and heard me crying. She was pretty sweet, getting down on her hands and knees and talking to me under the cubicle door. (I was slightly worried about her getting germs in her nice blonde hair.)

Anyway, I was feeling too much like a wobbly jelly to come out, so Verity went for help.

"Excuse me!" I heard her call out into the corridor. "But Rowan Love is in here and she's crying! And I don't know what to do! And someone needs to talk to her! And she's crying and everything! And–" etc., etc.

The person who came to her/my rescue turned out

to be Miss Boyle, who just happened to be click-clacking along in the corridor outside.

"Rowan, *please* won't you come out?" Miss Boyle asked me gently about a million times.

I didn't feel up to it till she added, "We could go and have a choc-chip cookie and a chat in the staffroom, if you like?"

Anyway, she was very cross about the graffiti going on in the Female Visitors' Toilets and says she's going to stand up in the next assembly on Monday and – without mentioning me or Verity and either of us crying – say it's *got* to stop.

Miss Boyle made me feel so much better that I *almost* starting telling her about how pretty much *everything* I did seemed to annoy *someone*, from my family to my best friend to my neighbours, and how I wasn't at all brave, and how I'd never be cool and ethereal like Libby-Mae Ferguson.

But then Miss Boyle asked how I was getting on with Georgie-who-is-NOT-a boy and I pulled a face, which she seemed to sense was not a good sign.

"The thing is, Georgie is a very, very shy girl, Rowan – which is why I paired her up with you, since you're so fun and kind!"

Ooh.

That sounded pretty good. A bit like something from the Fairy Philosophy!

Better stop – Miss Boyle's on her way back with the plaster. Ah, and a replacement cookie.

(Didn't I just say she was extra-specially lovely? I may have a small Hero Crush on her.)

Thursday 5.28 p.m.

Spooky!

Came home from school with Ally today, which was kind of nice *and* unusual, as she tends to wander home with her mate Sandie most days.

(This is *not* the spooky thing, by the way.)

It was kind of great to be able to tell her about my lousy day, and how Erin acted a bit "Oh, really?" rather than "Oh, wow, *no!*" like I'd've expected, when I told her why I'd come late to French class.

(*Also* not the spooky thing, by the way.)

Anyway, Ally was fooling around and saying stuff to make me laugh (like about how Erin sounded as flaky as my shoes!) when we stopped to look at a poster for the Chinese State Circus that I was going to with Erin and her mum and dad on Sunday.

(Yep – NOT the spooky thing yet.)

And who did I spot out of the corner of my eye?

Only Georgie-who-is-NOT-a-boy!

It was all the pink that did it. Now I love, *love*, LOVE pink . . . except for the sort that is so shocking pink it practically gives you a migraine.

And *that's* the shade of pink everyone in Georgie's family was wearing – except for her, of course.

"Hey, *that's* Georgie's mum!" said Ally, following my gaze.

Yep, I'd figured that out already. From Ally's previous description, I'd guessed who the woman wearing wet-look black leggings four sizes too small was. The shocking pink part of her outfit was a ruffled shirt and matching stilettos. In and around a buggy were three tiny girls – ranging from toddler to not-quite-toddler to baby – who were all dressed in shocking-pink frilly bits too.

In her dark school trousers and blazer and white school shirt, Georgie-who-is-NOT-a-boy looked like a panda being fostered by a family of flamingos.

Y'know, I was pretty sure Georgie had seen me but was pretending she hadn't.

Then something very strange-in-a-good-way happened. I got a little bit BRAVE!

Thanks to Miss Boyle's talk this morning and having Ally by my side, I walked right over and said "Hi!"

"Hi!" Georgie was forced to say back, blushing as red as the postbox we'd all stopped beside.

"Going to introduce me, love?" trilled her mum, above the chattering and whining of three small girls.

"This is Rowan," Georgie muttered in a weeny voice that was still nice to hear. "I'm doing that school project with her."

"Ooh!" cooed Georgie's mum, rifling quickly in her shopping bag and chucking three bags of Wotsits at the tiny pink whiners. "That's nice!"

"We've got to get together to come up with ideas for recycling," I told her.

"Yeah? Lovely! When're you doing that, then?" said Georgie's mum, looking all animated, while Georgie looked like she wished she was a turtle and could retract her head into her neck.

And *here's* the spooky bit: my mouth said something ALL on its own, without my brain even *thinking* it!

"Georgie could come round to mine on Saturday afternoon, if she likes! I just live along here a bit, on Palace Heights Road!"

From Georgie's expression, you'd think I'd suggested we offer her as a human sacrifice.

"Ooh, a play date! Lovely!" Georgie's mum cooed again through sugar-pink lips. "It'll do her a world of good to get out of the house instead of staying stuck inside, getting under my feet! I'm always telling her that she should get herself some friends to hang out with! What time?"

And so *that's* how I've found myself having my first "play date" since I was about six years old. . .

Thursday 7.02 p.m.

I've started knitting!

Check me out!!

Grandma just taught me after tea. Think she wanted to cheer me up after I realized that I would have to put my ballet pumps in the bin (RIP), as they had cracked so much they looked like the surface of a dried-out lake in a drought.

First, she told me that when *she* was young, people knitted stuff, and then when they got bored with their jumpers or whatever, they'd unravel them and knit them into something *else*.

Excellent recycling story!

So Grandma found some knitting needles of Mum's and then we looked in drawers and at the back of the airing cupboard till we found some old, hand-knitted kiddie jumpers and bingo! I have a project idea!!!

Well, I have a *scarf* idea, as I think that's all I'm going to be able to do for a start. I'm doing a long, skinny one in a silvery grey wool, inspired by Graham's wiggly lines on my bedroom wall.

No luck in finding Graham, by the way. So before he went to bed, Tor left out a saucer of lettuce leaves for him on my damp carpet*, in an attempt to woo him out of hiding.

* Most traces of orange paint have gone, thanks to my kind and slightly obsessive grandma spending all morning scrubbing away with carpet cleaner.

Thursday 10.30 p.m.
I can't stop knitting!

My skinny scarf is approximately one metre long (and about three centimetres wide).

Y'know, while I've been knitting, I've been thinking about stuff. And what I've thought is...

a) I am not going to be bugged by stupid graffiti written by stupid people. (Well, I'll try.)
b) My problem with Libby-Mae Ferguson is that I'm way too shy to talk to her (I am not worthy), and so I need to wangle a way for her to talk to me. I figure that if I wear my cool new scarf tomorrow, and

wander by her slowly, maybe she'll check it out (being so amazingly cool herself) and she'll say, "Hey! Where did you get that?" and I'll tell her, and then say casually, "By the way, is this fairy brooch yours?", and then she'll be utterly grateful and we'll be friends for ever. Possibly.

c) Maybe I haven't been a very good friend to Erin recently; I *have* been going on a lot about doing up my room and recycling projects and fairy websites and, er, Libby-Mae Ferguson and everything and maybe I haven't been asking how *she's* doing.

I will carry on knitting like a crazy knitting fiend and work on working out all the stuff above.

Oops, dropped a stitch. Three, actually.

Never mind! I'll just pretend it's part of some freestyle pattern.

FRIDAY

Friday 7.01 a.m.

Woke up just now to the sound of someone/something being sick. Got up fast and stepped into a sludge of regurgitated lettuce. (Nice one, Rolf.)

Friday 10.12 a.m.

I'm in the Female Visitors' Toilets. Have just doodled over the graffiti about me and Verity Melly in gold pen. Did swirls like in the artist Gustav Klimt's famous paintings. My art teacher, Mr Grayson, would be very impressed, if it wasn't sort of graffiti too and therefore technically against school rules.

Oh, and excellent news! The postman arrived with a World War II DVD box set this morning before I left for school – i.e., another competition which I WON!!

Won't be as useful and edible as the sausages, though.

Friday 12.48 p.m.

Lunch time was OK-ish with Erin. Planned not to talk about myself and to talk about *her* lots more, but in the end, Ingrid and Yaz sat with us and we all had to listen while Yaz spoke about the time she tried wearing her floppy fringe brushed over to the *other* side of her face and how that felt really weird.

"It's to do with my parting, Mum says," yakked Yaz. "Oh!"

I sort of woke up when she said "Oh!" in that semi-startled way.

"I didn't mean to mention, y'know, *mums* and whatever," said Yaz, looking flustered and glancing at me. Ingrid was looking at me too. Erin was looking at the ground.

It made me feel so confused that I said I had to go to the library (true) and left them to it.

It wasn't till I got here (the library) just now that I figured out what that bit of strangeness was all about – they were all freaked out about Mum not being around.

!!!

Has Erin been talking to Ingrid and Yaz about her? I mean, I wouldn't mind if she had, and made it sound OK, but from that reaction, I don't think they *do* think it's OK at all.

(*See* what I mean about people thinking it's weird

and not just quite interesting that she's not living with us at the moment?)

Anyway, I've decided to forget it, and I am now looking at the Find Your Inner Fairy website. And there is a NEWSFLASH on it! The news is very, *very* interesting; there is going to be a FAIRY FUN DAY in Trafalgar Square in two weeks' time!

It says here: "*It's going to be a day to celebrate all things fluffy and to spread a little fairy dust over the centre of London!!*"

I want to go! I want to go! I want to—

ALERT!!

Libby-Mae Ferguson and her two mates have just wandered into the library. Never mind my scarf: if she sees me looking at the Find Your Inner Fairy website, she will DEFINITELY realize I am a kindred spirit and come over to talk to me.

Then I could say, "Hey, have you seen that there's going to be a Fairy Fun Day soon?"

And she'll say, "Yeah? Hey, maybe we can go together!!"

And then we'll be friends for ever, for sure. I hope.

Friday 12.58 p.m.
Disaster.

Tried to lean casually sideways so that Libby-Mae Ferguson had an unhindered view of the Fairy Fun Day page in all its twinkly splendour, but my extra-long skinny scarf got caught in the wheels of the office chair I was sitting in and I ended up choking badly over the keyboard. Miss Whyte the librarian had to rescue me by snipping through my scarf with a large pair of scissors while shouting, "GIVE HER SPACE, EVERYONE!!!" very loudly.

By the time I could breathe properly again, Miss Whyte had shooed people out of the library, so I have no idea what Libby-Mae's reaction was. She probably wasn't overwhelmed by how cool or spiritual I seemed, I'm guessing.

I am now sitting with a reviving glass of water and piece of strawberry tart (from Miss Whyte's own lunch box), so it's not all bad.

Friday 6 p.m.

Have just spent the last half hour stroking something Dad brought home from work.

No, not a bent bike wheel in need of repair – a CAT!

A very fluffy black and white cat with no tail called (get this) FLUFFY!

Of all the names in the world . . . isn't that absolutely *spooky*?!

'Cause of that stuff about making your world more fluffy, on the Find Your Inner Fairy website, I mean? (Except when I said, "I can't *believe* she's called Fluffy!" downstairs just now, Linn *had* to ruin it by muttering, "IT'S ONE OF THE MOST COMMON CATS' NAMES OF THE LAST *CENTURY*, YOU MUPPET!!!")

Anyway, Dad got Fluffy from the people who have the shop next door to his. They said Fluffy and their Rottweiller weren't getting on, so Fluffy had to go (?). What else could Dad do but take her?

I don't understand how people can be so cruel and dump pets like they're rubbish. I mean, Fluffy is absolutely lovely, even if she *is* hissing and spitting at every furry member of the household that comes near her.

"Why's she got no tail?" asked Tor, confused by the fact that his hand stopped short when he was doing a stroke down the cat's back.

"BECAUSE SHE'S A BREED OF CAT KNOWN AS A MANX. THEY DON'T *HAVE* TAILS," said Linn, in her super-knowledgeable way. I was quite impressed.

"No, she's not, actually," Dad butted in. "The dog she lived with bit her tail off."

You've never heard so much "awwwwww!!!"ing at one time. Which was nice, considering that *right* before Dad turned up with Fluffy, there'd been a lot of "aaaarghh!!!"ing going on because Rolf was spotted running out of the back door with the last of the packets of Wall's sausages I was going to use to make a stew with tomorrow night*. (There were five empty plastic packets fluttering around the lawn.)

Though strangely, *Linn* wasn't aaaarghhhing, which made me wonder if she sort of *let* Rolf take all six packets of sausages out of the fridge. After my soup last weekend, she did say she'd "RATHER EAT GERBIL FOOD THAN ANYTHING *YOU* COOK, RO!"

Meanie.

* Wasn't sure how to make it anyway. I'd thought I'd just boil all thirty-six sausages in a large pot of water with a couple of carrots and some gravy granules. Would that have been OK? Will never know now. . .

Friday 11.10 p.m.

Can't get to sleep due to pneumatic-drill purring in my ears and excess fluff on my pillow (and cheek).

But I am *very* honoured that this cat has decided that my Ra-Ra-Raspberry room is the best in the house.

I also love the fact that from now on, if I'm having an un-fluffy moment, I can just cuddle our new pet for comfort and get an infusion (good vocabulary; tick!) of Fluffiness (ha!) in one firm squeeze.

By the way, the competitions and giveaways I entered in the *Hornsey Journal* this week were for...

- A year's supply of dandruff shampoo
- A mini food liquidizer
- A laptop (!!!)
- Bratz dolls Hawaiian Nail Salon

Obviously, I really, really would love to win the laptop, so I can look up stuff like the Find Your Inner Fairy website whenever I fancy.

After that, in descending order, would be the mini food liquidizer (may help me liquidize future sausage stews for the family); the dandruff shampoo (everyone needs shampoo, even though not everyone's got dandruff); and lastly the Bratz dolls Hawaiian Nail Salon.

The Bratz thing comes last, of course, 'cause no one in my family is the right age to play with it. It's also because Grandma once said that Bratz dolls' mouths reminded her of cats' bottoms.

By the way, I'm quite nervous about Georgie-who-is-NOT-a-boy coming tomorrow for our "play date", ho, ho, ho.

I mean, will she actually come? And *if* she comes, will she actually talk? Or will she just stare at me like I'm toxic again?

Maybe I should just hide under my duvet when Georgie rings the doorbell, like I did when I knew Dad was reading through my school report.

It would probably be a relief for both of us, even if it *does* mean no excellent recycling project ideas. . .

SATURDAY

Saturday 4.32 p.m.

Georgie-who-is-NOT-a-boy has just left.

I think our mad house blew her *mind*.

To be exact, I'd say she arrived horribly shy and left *less* shy but definitely bewildered.

It wasn't just the fact that our house is painted all in nuts colours inside and has Mum's random paintings and sculptures everywhere, it's cause it was more insanely crowded than normal this afternoon.

I gave her a quick guided tour, but she said absolutely nothing when I introduced her to Ally, who was in the living room watching telly with a whole bunch of mates (six!), plus three dogs (ours and Billy's pooch Precious).

She said nothing again when I got us drinks from the kitchen, and pointed to Linn, who was in deep, meaningful discussion with her mates Nadia, Mary and

Alfie (a very gorgeous boy, who I'd *definitely* go out with if I was as cool and ethereal as Libby-Mae Ferguson).

She said a bit *more* nothing as we delicately stepped over Frankie, Derek and Colin, all snoozling at different points on the stairs.

She did squeak a bit when she went to use our loo (Eddie was asleep in the sink), and gasped when she saw the row upon row of cages full of gerbilly/tweetery things in Tor's bedroom.

I think she was stunned back into total silence when we walked into *my* room, and came face to face with all the Ra-Ra-Raspberry and the wall-to-wall (-to-wall) reams of fairy lights.

The loudest she got was when Tor popped up from behind my bed like a boy-shaped meerkat. The noise she made was like a hamster-soft "eeek!" crossed with a gulp.

She really is just about the shyest person in the universe. . .

"Have you seen my snail?" Tor asked Georgie straight out.

He had a bendy dandelion in his hand. Georgie blinked at him and held on to her glass of juice very, very tightly.

"This is my brother, Tor. He's looking for a stray pet," I explained, realizing how bizarre my little brother looked. "The dandelion is bait."

(OK, so what I said might have sounded bizarre too, now I read it back. . .)

Georgie *still* said nothing, and looked like she might be up for saying nothing for *quite* a long time.

"Do you want to sit down?" I asked, ushering her towards the bed. She perched anxiously on the edge, like it might eat her.

Eeek . . . we'd *never* bond and work as a team like this!

And worse than that, thanks to the stress of all that silence, my inner panic goblin had begun to pad around in my chest.

Luckily, he was defeated by my superhero little brother!!

"Do *you* have a pet?" Tor asked Georgie, ignoring the fact that she hadn't answered his first question.

"No," Georgie answered. (One small, short word, but least it was a start.)

"Why not?"

"Um, dunno. . ." Georgie frowned, thrown by five-year-old logic.

"Do you have any brothers or sisters?"

Wow, Tor was in a madly talkative mood for him.

"Um, I, uh, have three little sisters."

"What are their names?"

It was great – I didn't have to say a word! It was pretty weird that Tor was suddenly so chatty. I mean, normally, he just communicates telepathically (good vocabulary; tick!) with all the pets.

I don't know . . . maybe 'cause he somehow sensed he was in the presence of someone even *quieter* than himself, he suddenly came over like a cutting-edge TV interviewer.

"Um . . . McKenzie, Sapphire and Romany."

"Oh, *I* remember! My other sister said that you play football!" Tor announced.

OK, so he must have overheard the conversation I'd had with Ally after I'd first met Georgie. Though the fact that she was wearing an Arsenal football top today might have helped him guess that she was a football fan.

"Mmm," nodded Georgie.

"And Ally said your mum always wears really tight trous–"

!!!

Whoa – wrong time for Tor to get chatty. It seemed like a good moment to join in with the conversation.

"Where did your parents get those names from?" I asked quickly.

"A celeb magazine," she muttered.

"Yours, too?"

"Um, no . . ." she said hesitantly, "I was named after a footballer my dad used to love called Georgie Best." (Hey! That last bit was a whole sixteen-word sentence, if you include the 'um'! Talk about progress!!)

I kind of started to relax a bit then and told Georgie all about *our* names: that Linn was short for Linnhe, the name of a loch in Scotland; *I* was named after a particular tree my mum loved; Ally was named after Alexandra Palace, which we can see from the attic; and Tor ended up Tor after some famously spooky/ spiritual hill in Glastonbury, where the world-famous music festival happens ever year.

I asked her about her dad – he's a soldier and she doesn't see him for months on end when he's working abroad. I told her that Mum was working abroad too and we hadn't seen her for ages either; and Georgie didn't seem fazed, thanks to her dad's job, I suppose.

I tried speaking to her about school and friends, but only got as far as a few facts about the other Alexandra Hill buddies.

Bianca's got a bit of a temper, apparently, "'Cause of

people tending to think she's about *eight*, I guess," Georgie said with a shrug.

Yusuf hides out in the ICT suite all the time. "He got locked in one time after school and didn't even notice," she told me.

And Omar spends most of his breaks looking at old Manchester United annuals. "So he'll be fluent at explaining corners and the offside rule in English, then?!" I grinned at Georgie.

Though she got the joke and grinned back, I thought that the lack of friend-related info was maybe a bit weird. That's until I remembered Georgie's mum going on about Georgie staying in all the time – I suspected that maybe she didn't have too many mates from school (or anywhere else, for that matter) and shut up.

Anyway, after talking names and buddies and faraway parents, Georgie seemed to relax a bit too (her knuckles weren't quite so white where she was gripping the glass). And so to make her feel more at home, I gave her a detailed guided tour of my room.

I showed her stuff like my designs for an angel dress for when I hang-glide over the Himalayas, the daisy rectangle where Johnny Depp used to be, my scrapbook of Johnny Depp stuff, the section of my dressing table full of ONLY stripy socks and tights (other patterns live in a different section), the boxes under my bed full of craft bits, and Fluffy, who's taken to sleeping in my pants drawer, as she's still a bit nervous of the other pets (i.e., she's still hissing and spitting at them).

Then – get this – Georgie picked up my *Hornsey Journal* prize box set of World War II DVDs and said "Oooh!!" in the sort of way *I* say "Oooh!" when I see something covered in sequins.

"What?" I asked.

"I like history" was all Georgie mumbled, as her eyes skimmed the back of the box.

I suddenly thought about Georgie's big pink mum, and all Georgie's shrieky small siblings, and realized her home probably wasn't the sort of place you could have a stimulating chat about the French Revolution or the Roman Invasion or whatever.

"You can have it, if you want!" I told her.

Wow. From the way Georgie's face lit up, it was as if I'd offered her a lifetime supply of chocolate-covered raisins.

Anyway, while she was glowing (and Tor was still scrabbling around on the carpet) I said that maybe we should get down to thinking up some recycling ideas. But Georgie looked at her watch and said she had to go

141

'cause her nana and grandpa were coming for tea.

That was a bit of a pain, since it was the whole point of her coming round.

Then again, I was *very* pleased that I'd made Georgie so happy, mainly because I'd thought the only other person who might like that box set was my grandad. (But as he died quite a while ago, I guess that just leaves Georgie.)

Saturday 5.23 p.m.

Tor yelled a few minutes ago and held up Graham the snail.

I whooped along with him till he started to look a bit worried, 'cause Graham wasn't oozing out of his shell like you'd have expected.

Squinting at the dried-up snot-a-like inside the shell, I realized that Graham was pretty much *dead*. I guess that was to be expected, as there's a lot of stuff in my room, but none of it is snail-friendly vegetation.

But 'cause I didn't want to upset Tor, I told him Graham had probably developed agoraphobia (fear of open spaces – good vocabulary; tick!) since he'd been lost and was simply too scared to come out.

Then I did my most thoughtful, doctorly face and

advised Tor to leave Graham alone in his box overnight to chill out.

I'll get Ally to help me search in the garden for a replacement snail as soon as Tor's asleep.

SUNDAY

Sunday 10.55 a.m.

Lying in the bath writing this. Have to be careful, as I got one gingham corner of my journal wet a second ago when I lost concentration, i.e., when Eddie the cat leant over from his bed, i.e., the sink, and swatted at the knitting needles I've stuck in my bun to stop my hair unravelling.

(Rule No. 16: *I will NOT drop journals or other important documents in the bath*.)

Actually, I'm just about to get ready for the Chinese State Circus, and I'm VERY EXCITED. That's because the *last* time I saw the show, I had a *huge* Hero Crush on the *entire* troupe of Chinese girls, who came out in national costume and spun a whole bunch of plates on sticks each so that it looked *exactly* like a flock of vibrating butterflies were fluttering about the ring. It was so incredibly pretty it made me cry.

I can't wait to see them again. (And cry again.)

It'll be great too, because I get to hang out with Erin properly for the first time this week, without Ingrid and Yaz butting in with floppy fringe conversations or going silent on me when I come over.

I mean, we'll be hanging out with her dad Dave and her mum Gillian, of course. But they are so nice and funny and everything that it's not like it's a form of hanging-out-with-someone's-parents embarrassment torture or anything. Well, maybe for Erin, but not for me.

By the way, I had an *amazing* idea for a recycling project ten minutes ago!

At first, I *had* toyed with making loads of long skinny scarves, but then changed my mind, because . . .

a) I realized most jumpers these days come from Marks & Spencer's and are not hand-knitted and cannot therefore be unravelled and *re*-knitted, and . . .
b) I'd gone off the idea since I got strangled.

But my new *amazing* idea happened over breakfast when Ally told me that she was going to meet Billy and his dog in the park this afternoon. She joked that since Billy's mum had taken their poodle to the dog groomer's yesterday, it meant the newly shorn Precious was probably going to be even *more* shivery and yappity and bad-tempered than normal.

As I waded through my Weetabix, I found myself picturing Precious's spindly white legs, all a-tremble in the slightest breeze blowing in the park.

Then I thought of the stripy purple and black lurex tights I'd picked out for my circus-visiting outfit today, only to realize they were ripped.

Ta-*DA!*

A poodle. . .

Ripped tights. . .

I mean, it's *SO* obvious!!

I'm going to make Precious a pair (OK, *two* pairs) of *teeny doggy leg warmers!*

They will be my prototype, and I will display them on our stall at the Raise Awareness of Recycling in the Community environmental event thingy in Hornsey Town Hall Square in a fortnight's time. Maybe Precious could model them! (Wouldn't try it with Rolf or Winslet; Rolf would probably eat them and Winslet would growl at me if I tried to put them on her.)

Wow, I can't *wait* till Monday to tell Georgie and Miss Boyle!!!

P.S. Tor is very happy with Graham Take Two, who was slithering down his arm towards his beans on toast last time I looked. (Graham Take One is buried under the rhododendron bush by the shed. Rolf was watching me while I was doing it, and I worried he might dig Graham up. But then two seconds after I finished, Derek wandered over and did a poo on the exact spot, so I think the burial site is safe.)

Sunday 4.56 p.m.
Here's my review of the Chinese State Circus. . .

First half: "*A dazzling, breathtaking display of artistry and acrobatics! A feast for the eyes and the senses!*" (Good vocabulary; tick!)

Second half: "*Blurry. . .*"

OK, here's all that *again*, with some illuminating detail to help explain. . .

First half: I wore my flowery tights instead, with my denim shorts, Mum's hippy smock top, and my excellent beanie with the luminous beads sewn on.

Erin's mum Gillian was very sweet — like always — and said she loved my hat a lot, and passed around an unfeasible (good use of vocabulary; tick!) amount of chocolate and popcorn.

Erin's dad Dave was very funny — like

always – nicking my beanie and trying it on, buying me and Erin kiddie light-up wands from a circus kiosk, and grabbing us both tight in fake alarm when the acrobats' acts got hairily scary. (I giggled when he did that; Erin tutted.)

So, the first half of the circus was very good (like before).

Me and Erin clapped and gasped and wowed (like before).

And then the interval came, and it all went wrong, starting with the fateful words:

"Still up for going to the ice rink for your birthday?"

That was *me* speaking, and it didn't seem very fateful at the time.

'Cause it was the interval, me and Erin and Erin's mum Gillian were in the very long queue for the loos-in-a-lorry. (It's weird to think that a bunch of toilets go on tour with all those brilliant performers and all that amazing scenery and costumes and props and stuff.)

I had to turn around to speak to Erin, seeing as she was behind me in the queue. (Erin's mum Gillian was standing behind Erin, happily reading through the programme while we waited and inched forward.)

"Yeah . . . I think that would be pretty good," said Erin, sounding to me as if she wasn't all *that* sold on the ice-skating idea all of a sudden.

"We could always go to the movies instead, if you fancy?" I suggested. "We've never got round to seeing that new Pixar movie and I'm sure it's still on at the Muswell Hill Odeon!"

Like I say, I have this condition of the mouth where it sometimes starts talking before my brain has had a chance to say, "Er, are you *sure* about this?"

And right on cue, about a nanosecond after I spoke, my brain flashed up the confusing image of a cinema ticket stuck to Erin's pinboard in her bedroom. That was the *same* nanosecond that Erin stared at me like a very timid piglet spotting a rabid wolf, and the *same* nanosecond Erin's mum Gillian glanced up sharply from the programme with an expression like a thunderous cloud with a migraine.

What had I *done*?!

For a slither of a moment I wondered if I'd gone *mad* and accidentally babbled satanic messages without realizing.

"I, uh, don't really fancy that film, actu – *oh*!!"

As Erin's spoke, her mum Gillian interrupted with a mighty elbow to her side.

"*Enough*, Erin!!" she snapped.

Phew . . . I was slightly relieved to see that the thunderous-cloud-with-a-migraine expression was aimed at *Erin* for some reason, not me. But only slightly, 'cause I wasn't at *all* used to seeing laid-back Gillian doing stern and grumpy.

(The queue moved forward, and I ended up walking backwards up a few steps towards the loos-in-the-lorry.)

"*Mum!*" mumbled Erin, looking annoyed and uncomfortable and agitated all at once, and like she might want to run off into the bushes in Ally Pally park, given half a chance.

"Erin, I'm *not* covering up for you any more!!" barked her mum, who never, *ever* barked. "It's not fair on Rowan!"

"*What's* not fair on Rowan?" I asked, taking another few backwards, upwards steps closer to the loo.

Mmm . . . my panic goblin was giving himself a nice big stretch in my chest.

I noticed that Erin's face had turned as red as the roses on my tights. She was now staring at the rickety metal steps as if they were made of special magnets that were pulling her eyeballs down.

"I've seen it already. The film, I mean. I saw it a couple

150

of weekends ago. I . . . I went with Ingrid and Yaz."

My mouth went into limbo, but my brain worked overtime, flying a thought as quick as a frisbee my way.

That had been the afternoon I ended up in the park with Dad and Tor and Ally, 'cause Erin hadn't turned up, and her mum had said she was out with her dad "shopping".

Yeah, while *I* was getting a split lip (not that Tor meant it), Erin had sloped off to the movies with Ingrid and Yaz, and left her mum to make up an excuse to fob me off with. No wonder her dad Dave was as confused as a fish with a skateboard when I mentioned it in the paint shop last week.

"You didn't come to help me paint my room. . ." I said sadly, backing into the lorry, where cubicle doors were slamming shut and banging open, and there was a hurly-burly of splashing taps and whooshing hand driers.

Maybe it was the fact that her eyes stayed firmly on the steps, or maybe it was 'cause her mum gave her another get-on-with-it! nudge, but I suddenly knew that Erin *hadn't* had a cold last weekend.

As I hurried into an open cubicle and shut the door on her guilty face, I knew Erin had *actually* had a bad case of got-better-things-to-do-itis. Which obviously could only be cured with a dose of Ingrid and Yaz.

I've never had a more miserable wee. . .

I hardly even registered the voice on the tannoy telling us to get back to our seats, till I shuffled out to wash my hands and found Erin's mum Gillian steering me back towards the big tent by rubbing her hand on my back. (Erin was trailing somewhere behind, probably dragging my heart with her on her shoe, like a bit of stray toilet paper.)

And so to the second half of the circus: like I say, blurry. Guess why.

At the end – when the applause had stopped and the lights came on – Erin mumbled (get this), "I didn't mean anything; they asked me, and I just liked hanging out with them for a change."

It wasn't too flattering, to know that I was the sort of person it was good to have a change from.

And though Gillian had rolled her eyes when Erin was talking and Dave mimed strangling her behind her back, the sympathetic looks my (supposed) best friend's parents were strobing my way made me feel bad instead of better.

So in the end, it turned out to be me who ran off into the bushes in Ally Pally park.

And now I'm back home in my room, hiding out from my family. (Dad, Ally and Linn are in the back garden, watching Tor trying to coax Graham the Snail Take Two over an obstacle course he's made out of cake trays and wooden spoons. How can I interrupt that kind of happiness?)

Sunday 6.07 p.m.
Only managed to eat seven peas and a noodle, due to sadness overload.

Told Dad I had a tummy-ache so he was cool about me skipping tea after that and coming up to my room.

Flipped my journal open to the back and flopped my head down on my inner fairy, in the hope of finding some comfort. But who knew glitter was so sharp? It now looks like I've tried to sandpaper my forehead.

I don't like today.

Sunday 10.15 p.m.
I *can't* lose my best friend.

I don't have a zillion, like Ally, or even a handful, like Linn, where losing one wouldn't be a disaster.

I have only *one* best friend and I don't know what I would do without her!

I need to do something drastic.

And I have ABSOLUTELY decided what that something is going to be. . .

WEEK 3

MONDAY

Monday 8.35 a.m.

You should have seen how my family all stared at me this morning when I came down for breakfast; like I was a flesh-eating *zombie*, for goodness' sake.

It wasn't really the reaction I was hoping for. . .

"*BOO!*" I said.

Nobody said anything back.

In fact, the only sounds were some song zinging away on the radio, Rolf snurfling hopefully around under the table for crumbs, and Dad coughing, as if he was choking on his toast after a sudden shock.

Tor broke the silence first. He said, "Is it you?"

Not surprisingly, I said, "Yes."

Then it was Dad's turn.

"You – *cuh, cuh!*" he coughed. "You look very . . . *cuh, cuh!* very nice, Rowan!"

I said a sort of self-conscious thank you, and helped

myself to a piece of toast from the mound in the middle of the table.

"Where's Linn?" I asked, spreading on some peanut butter.

"She had to leave early – *cuh, cuh!* Her class is going on a field trip today," Dad coughed some more.

I knew that, actually, but I was just double-checking that the coast was clear. 'Cause if she'd been here, Linn would've been shouting, "ARE THOSE <u>MY</u> SHOES?!" at me.

But what was I supposed to do?

I didn't have any shoes that were *remotely* sensible, and all *her* shoes were exceptionally sensible. *And* we've the same size feet. *And* she doesn't ever *wear* these particular sensible black slip-ons I'd just sensibly slipped on.

(Even if I'd asked her if I could borrow them – and *not* just sneaked into her room and taken them this morning – she'd still've said no. It's not her fault. I think Linn just has to *look* at me and her mind automatically screams "NO!!")

"Why?" asked Ally, which threw me for a second. (Why had I asked where Linn was? Or was the why for *why* did I look like this. . .)

"I need a change," I said casually, though I didn't exactly feel very casual.

The thing is, I don't NEED a change, I just need to fit in with my best friend more.

It's not just a sudden thing.

It's not as if last night I was struck by this lightning bolt of certainty (good vocabulary; tick!), where I instantly understood that the way I dress sometimes embarrasses Erin.

I think I've *always* pretty much known that she thinks the way I look is too kooky.

It's just that last night it hit me that to be a better friend, I need to *stop* embarrassing her.

And to do that, the new, improved, non-annoying me is going to have to look a *lot* like Erin.

Yep, I am determined to look and act more NORMAL* (new Rule No. 17).

And if Erin appreciates the effort I have made to go all normal for her, then *maybe* she won't be so tempted to let Ingrid and Yaz steal her away from me. . .

---

*It took an unexpectedly long time to get ready this morning. It took *ages* to find the one plain black pair of tights I knew I had somewhere (tucked in the corner of the bookshelves, don't know why); *more* ages to unpick the pink sequins from my deep-purple hairband, and even *more* ages to blow-dry my fringe so it was suitably floppy (it covered the sandpapered patch of my forehead at least).

Even finding pants this morning took for ever, because I was trying to find a pair that wasn't covered in fur. (Tor says cats shed more when they're stressed, and Fluffy is *definitely* stressed, going by the amount of hissing and spitting she's doing when any of the other pets wander into my room for a friendly sniff.)

Nearly forgot to take off my nail varnish too. Couldn't go to school with that on because . . .

a)   it is *slightly* against school rules (though I usually just stick my hands in my pockets around teachers), and
b)   Ingrid and Yaz would never be seen with alternating green and turquoise nail varnish.

Monday 10.02 a.m.

I'm in the far-left cubicle of the Female Visitors' Toilets. (Hey, it's getting to be like my office!)

So far, so OK . . . my new rule about looking and acting more normal seems to be going down well with Erin. She was pretty stunned and amazed when she saw me come into the playground, and said I looked *way* different. (Result!)

Actually, 'cause of Erin's reaction and this morning's family stare-a-thon, I kind of expected *more* people might gawp at me, but then sitting in assembly, it dawned on me that it hadn't happened because no one really *recognized* me.

!!!

By the way, assembly was interesting. Mr Bashir, the head teacher, got up and said all his usual blah, blah,

blah school stuff, and then he introduced Miss Boyle, who spoke (without mentioning any names) about the graffiti in the toilets, and said that people have to be aware of the fact that while *they* might think they're just being funny, they are *actually* being cruel in a very cowardly, anonymous way. (You tell it like it is, Miss Boyle!!)

Then Mr Bashir stood back up and added that he wouldn't tolerate bullying or discrimination in *any* form, including graffiti – and (deep, gruff voice) *ANYONE* caught vandalizing the toilets in this way would be hanged, drawn and quartered (or something similar).

While he was talking I sneaked a look at Verity Melly, sitting two rows in front of me with her mates, and saw that she was glowing as red as I felt. (Hey, everyone! It's *us*! *We're* the ones who've been graffiti'd!!)

I just sat there and hoped there weren't any rogue heat-seeking missiles in the vicinity or me and Verity would be blown to smithereens for *sure*.

Monday 11.10 a.m.
In chemistry just now. Feeling a bit itchy. Guess I should stop Fluffy sleeping in my pants drawer.

Monday 11.12 a.m.

Rowan Fluffy Love? Very silly and cute! Though might not work if I ended up being a forty-five-year-old court judge.

Monday 12.45 p.m.

I've just been online in the library.

I was playing around with making a website advertising pet leg warmers, but accidentally (on purpose) logged on to the Find Your Inner Fairy website instead. And – get *this* – I realized that the Fairy Fun Day in Trafalgar Square is on the *same* Saturday as the exhibition about the environment and recycling and stuff at the Town Hall Square in Crouch End.

Boo!!!

I mean, Libby-Mae Ferguson is BOUND to be going. Not fair! What can I do?! Maybe I can ask Miss Boyle if it's OK for me not to be at the exhibition. . . Georgie would be all right on her own with the pet leg warmers, wouldn't she? Well, she'd be too shy to talk about them, I suppose, but she could just hold them up and waft them around a bit. Though they might just look like floppy bits of old tights if she did that. . .

May have to work on that plan.

Speaking of plans, I amazed myself by accidentally

having a very *cunning* one at lunch today. I spotted two seats together on a really crowded table in the dining hall, and led Erin right over to them. See what I did there? No free seats meant *no* Ingrid and Yaz joining us. And *no* Ingrid and Yaz joining us means no one trying to take my best friend away from me.

Must stick to this new and excellent plan!

Monday 12.49 p.m.
Just had a very, very nuts thought. Did Ingrid and Yaz do the mean graffiti about me?!

No, they wouldn't.

Monday 12.50 p.m.
Would they?

Monday 5.54 p.m.
It was the flesh-eating zombie thing all over again when I met up with Miss Boyle and everyone to walk to the Reuse and Recycle Centre earlier this afternoon.

"Well, that's a *very* different look for you, Rowan!" Miss Boyle said cheerfully, after taking a second or two to realize it was *me* standing in front of her.

"Did someone *dare* you to look normal?" William Smith teased me.

I told him to shut up or I'd find some more potential turbo boosters at the recycling centre and attach them to the inside of his nostrils. (He thought that was pretty funny.)

Verity – nibbling on a piece of her own hair – told me that my *hair* looked "really, really, y'know, I mean, well, *nice!*" this way, which worried me a bit, in case she meant it looked quite tasty.

Marlon just stared at me, which was a bit freaky. The last couple of weeks, it hasn't bothered me that he's a laid-back, ultra-quiet person, since I have one of those in my family (Tor). But the staring sort of reminded me that Marlon is a bit unknown and edgy; that he's capable of supergluing head teachers in their rooms, which is kind of freaky. . .

But forget them: *Georgie's* reaction was completely brilliant. When I walked into the educational Portakabin, she gazed *right* past me and then asked Miss Boyle if I was coming today!!!

Can you believe that? There was me thinking she was a *boy*, and now here *she* was, thinking I was normal!

Anyway, apart from helping sort out mistaken identities, Miss Boyle was all eager to hear our excellent ideas so far to help Raise Awareness of Recycling in the Community.

"But we haven't got one, Rowan!" Georgie whispered to me, all alarmed.

"Oh, yes, we *do*!" I whispered back, with what I hoped was a reassuring grin.

I thought Georgie looked more alarmed than reassured. But then Georgie *always* looks a bit alarmed, I realized. (Being surrounded by so much kiddly screaming and migraine pink at home probably makes her live on her nerves.)

"Do we?"

Georgie blinked her long, dark eyelashes at me hopefully, like she was silently begging me to make it all right. Her expression reminded me of Rolf when he's sitting beside his empty food bowl and gazing beseechingly at you (usually two hours early for tea).

"Trust me," I said, smiling a secret smile at Georgie and feeling kind of protective towards her.

It dawned on me that maybe she didn't have much confidence and was shy because she hadn't many friends, or maybe she hadn't many friends because she didn't have much confidence and was shy.

Well, *that* and the fact that she dressed like a boy and was well into world history and not Topshop. . .

Whatever, I remembered what Miss Boyle had said about me being fun and kind and realized all of a sudden that I wanted to be a really *great* buddy to Georgie. And maybe she especially deserved that for being just about the only person in the world not to bat an eyelid at the idea of Mum being far, far away. . .

"Who wants to go first?" Miss Boyle smiled.

"Me and Omar are good to go!" yelped William, saluting her (*told* you he was crazy).

So here's what they'd come up with: a leaflet that lets people know about the Reuse and Recycle Centre. Miss Boyle thought that was excellent (specially since they'd already designed it). She said that was a 9/10 effort.

She also said Verity and Bianca's jumble sale was a 9/10, because it was a very valid way to recycle.

Marlon and Yusuf came up with a bag bag, i.e., a little bag that you shove all the plastic bags in that you want to reuse. Miss Boyle went *wild* for that ("10/10!").

"So what about *you* two girls?" said Miss Boyle, finally turning to me and (a frightened) Georgie.

It was my big moment.

I took out my four stripy tubes and laid them out on the table.

Everyone looked at them, and then looked at me.

Their expressions were more "Huh?" than "Wow!" Or in Omar's case, whatever the Somalian equivalent is of "Huh?" and "Wow!"

"Bits of tights?" said Miss Boyle, with just a weeny hint of confusion.

My panic goblin suddenly sprinted across my chest, and I realized how *lame* my idea must seem to them, lying all floppy and lifeless on the table, so I asked if me and Georgie could nip across to the office Portakabin and get something.

"Um, of course!" said Miss Boyle, shrugging.

"What are we doing?" Georgie asked, as I hurried across to the first yellow-high-visibility-vest staff member I could see.

"We need to borrow one of that bloke's toys," I told her, probably sounding like I was making no sense. (Panic goblins have a habit of messing with your words, I find.)

What I *actually* meant was that I was hoping I could borrow one of the old soft toys racked up on the wrought-iron bench by the office, so I could use it as a leg warmer model.

"Maybe that rhino, or that Shrek," I thought aloud. "Which one do you think would suit leg warmers more?"

Before Georgie could answer, or I had a chance to ask the staff member, I saw something that made me go "Eeeep!"

'Cause there on the bench, huddled between a Woody from *Toy Story* and a baby doll with its eyes pushed in was. . .

"What's wrong?!" asked Georgie, freezing alongside me.

"It's . . . it's Sir Timothy Nutkins! No kidding!!" I gasped, making a little bit less sense to my poor, confused buddy.

So to cut a long, rambling story short (something I'm not great at doing), I ended up coming back home with Erin's childhood best friend PLUS a box full of all the tiny squirrel bits and bobs and ornaments that used to be on Erin's shelves! (The nice people in the yellow vests said they'd kept them to one side, as they were too cute to crush.)

But what on earth were Erin's squirrelly bits *doing* there?

I rang Erin's house the second I stumbled through the front door and dumped my rescued stuff down.

"Well, I *know* Erin did pack her squirrels away, but I don't think she'd have wanted to throw them *out!*" said Erin's mum Gillian, when she answered the phone. "Her dad must have scooped them up by accident when he was taking some things to the recycling centre. . ."

That was EXACTLY what *I* thought. And Gillian promised me she'd ask Erin (who wasn't home yet) and her dad Dave (who also wasn't home yet), and get Erin to call me back.

The thing is, she hasn't called yet, but then she might be having her tea, or been abducted by aliens or something.

P.S. When I finally got round to explaining it, I could tell that everyone thought the pet leg warmer idea was pants. (Miss Boyle called it "Mmm . . . interesting!", in that way that sounds kind but technically means "rubbish".) Sorry, Georgie.

1/10.

Monday 8.14 p.m.

No call back from Erin yet.

Should I phone her? Or will that seem like I'm pestering her? Uh-oh – I don't want to be a pestering friend. . .

It's not late – maybe she'll still call.

In the meantime, me and Fluffy been having quite an excellent time. Fluffy, because I moved her food and water bowls plus a litter tray into the bedroom so that she doesn't have to mingle with the other pets. And me? Well, I've been having an excellent time because I didn't *just* come home with the box of squirrels from the Reuse and Recycle Centre; I also picked up the most AMAZING frame! It's big and GOLD, with twirls and swirls, and it was quite hard to carry home, 'cause of it being so big and heavy and awkward and everything. Luckily, it has no glass or backing board to it (which was why it was dumped, I guess) so I put my head through it and wore it across my chest like a giant gold frame-shaped bag on the way home.

(Mr and Mrs Misery-Guts were out in their garden, and tutted at the sight of me with my piled-high squirrelly box and my big frame. Not fair! They hadn't even *noticed* that the rest of me looked sensible and un-tut-worthy!!)

OK, so I was thinking what to do with my frame, when I came up with an extremely interesting idea (I think).

Because there's no glass in it, you don't *have* to put flat stuff inside. I mean, I can pin anything I fancy to the wall (like maybe my first ballet shoes from when I was three, or my jumble sale top hat) and then just PLACE the frame around it.

Voila – instant 3D art.

!!!

Right, so while I haven't decided what to put in my new frame for *sure*, it *is* A3 – exactly the same size as my old Johnny Depp poster – so for the moment I've stuck it up on the original nail and now have a framed picture of my rectangle of daisy wallpaper. Ha!

Y'know, I think I'll try and collect more of these glass-less frames, in all sizes.

Maybe I can find a weeny one, and pin the broken-wing fairy brooch inside it, right by my bed.

'Cause it's taken me *so* long to try (and fail) to give it back to Libby-Mae Ferguson that I don't know if I *should* now.

How come?

Well, I mean, if I say to her, "I think this is *yours*," then she might say, "Where did you find it?" and then I'll have to tell her I saw her drop it, and then she'll say, "But that was two *weeks* ago. . .!"

Then I'll bet she'll think I'm some mad stalker who's been holding on to her stuff 'cause I *idolize* her or something.

(Yes, I realize some bits of that sentence are true.)

Hmm.

I'll just tuck the fairy brooch into the corner of the gold frame here for now, and think about that later* (probably when I'm thirty-seven).

---

* I know, I *know* . . . Rule No. 10 is the "shalt not steal" thingymee. Don't remind me.

TUESDAY

Tuesday 4.45 a.m.

I woke up a few minutes ago with my nose about three centimetres from the framed daisy wallpaper.

And with my liquid eyeliner in my hand. . .

After blinking for a while in the dawn light, I sussed that I must have been sleepwalking. Then I spotted this smudgy, hard-to-read black eyeliner *scrawl* that I'd done directly on the wall. Well, directly on to the patch of daisies in the frame.

The sleep-scrawl read:

"*RED THE ROOLS.*"

???

I stepped back (right on to Fluffy's paw – sorry!), thought for a second (while rubbing the clawed bit of my ankle), and realized that . . .

a)   my subconscious was trying to tell me something *important*, and

b)   it couldn't spell very well.

While I was mulling over the fact that it had also used up all my eyeliner, something in my brain clicked: my confused subconscious was advising me that to stick to my RULES better, I need to READ them every day.

In other words, I need to have them in front of me in black and white.

Better still, I need to see them in *pale pink* (I have a thick sheet of coloured card under my bed) and *raspberry* (I have a delicious glitter gel pen that's practically the same colour as the walls).

And my Raspberry Rules will have pride of place in my gorgeous gold frame!!

Will do it straight away, since I'll never get back to sleep now.

Tuesday 8.35 a.m.

Bit of a mad rush.

Dad came and woke me up at 8.15 a.m. I'd got as far as *"I will ALWAYS finish what I start"* (Rule No. 7) when I must have dozed off on the rug. He said it was pretty funny – he thought I'd dyed my hair black with a white streak in it (possible, in my non-sensible days), but it was just Fluffy, curled up round my head.

By the way, Linn was OK about the shoes I "borrowed".

Shock!!!

Well, it's not actually such a big shock – Ally heard Grandma telling Linn yesterday that I was experimenting with a new look (i.e., one she approved of*), and that it might be nice for Linn to help me out by donating the shoes that she clearly didn't wear anyway.

By the way, I'm writing this on my side of the kitchen table, and I can see that Linn is pretending to read one of her coursework books. But really, I can tell she's subtly staring over, because I can feel her eyes boring into me like Tor's finger in mashed potato when he's food-sculpting.

I think my new sensible look is confusing her.

Ooh, I quite *like* the idea of confusing her!

Must scoot to school – have a squirrel to deliver. . .

---

* Don't think Grandma would have been so understanding if the new look I'd been trying out really WAS black hair with white streaks.

Tuesday 8.55 a.m.
Uh-oh, uh-oh, uh-oh. . .

Something went *very* badly wrong just now.

I came into the playground and saw Erin over by the corner of the gym building and went rushing towards her, pulling Sir Timothy Nutkins out of my bag with an accompanying "TA-NAAA!!!"

What I *didn't* see till I was closer was that Ingrid and Yaz were standing *just* out of my line of vision, around the corner of the gym.

"What's *that* thing?" Yaz laughed, but not in a funny way.

"It's Erin's!!" my mouth blurted out, before my brain had time to tell it that Erin looked *horrified*, and that I had instantly failed Rule No. 17, i.e., to *look and act more NORMAL*.

(Stupid, stupid mouth.)

"Are you *kidding*? What are you *on* about, Ro?" Erin laughed, also in a non-funny way.

How incredibly *dumb* did I feel, hovering there holding a fluffy squirrel in a waistcoat in the middle of the air?

And with three sets of girls' eyes staring at me as if I was a complete freak?

(*Did* Ingrid and Yaz write that grafitti?)

BUT I was saved by Marlon Trueman.

My hero!

At *just* the right moment (i.e., the moment I was self-combusting through sheer shame) he came ambling over to me, hands in his pockets, glanced at me and Sir Timothy Nutkins – as if seeing a girl in the playground holding a stuffed squirrel in the air was the most normal, dull thing in the world – and said, "Miss Boyle wants us all to come help her do some stuff in the art room after lunch. Pass it on."

I could have kissed him.

Well, not *really*, but you know what I mean.

Um . . . better go, actually. It's awfully quiet outside of this loo cubicle. I think I might have missed the sound of the bell, as usual.

Tuesday 12.57 p.m.

I have just finished folding two hundred warm leaflets about the Reuse and Recycle Centre.

They were warm because they'd all just *flooped* out of the colour photocopier in the art resource room.

I wasn't the only one doing it, of course. There was Miss Boyle, and William (since the leaflets are *his* project, as he kept reminding us over and *over* again) and Verity ("Should I put more leaflets on *this* pile? Or that pile? Or maybe start a *new* pile? Or—" etc., etc.). Then there was Marlon. The whole time we were printing and folding, I kept catching him staring at me (spook!). Maybe he couldn't get the vision of me waving a squirrel around out of his head *after* all?

"Fantastic! Well done, everyone!" Miss Boyle had said after the last leaflet joined Verity's latest pile. "We're all ready for Saturday now!"

Saturday is the jumble sale, by the way. Well, the Big Bring-&-Swap Party, as it's now known. That's Miss Boyle's twist on it; make it a free event where people take along what they don't want and swap it for what they do. (*I* came up with the name, by the way.) It's going to happen in the main hall at Alexandra Hill School. We're all going to help set it up, and hand out William and Omar's leaflets there.

"Remember to tell all your friends and family to come along!" Miss Boyle beamed, as she began packing leaflets into a box.

That's when I felt a bit flat, to be honest. I somehow didn't think I'd be taking a friend, since Erin had been acting all cool with me since the squirrel incident in the playground.

I mean, she gave me a quick, no-eye-contact "sorry" in maths, followed by this rushed, whispered explanation about how she just wasn't into "kid" stuff any more, and had actually ASKED her dad Dave to take Sir Timothy Nutkins and her box full of squirrel stuff to the dump when he was dropping off an old toilet or two in his plumber's van.

But hey; couldn't Erin – being my so-called best friend and everything – have saved me from wanting to curl up and die in front of Ingrid and Yaz and just *admitted* Sir Timothy Stupid Nutkins had once upon a time been *hers*?!

(Answer: no, obviously.)

After that, the atmosphere had been so *tense* between us that at break time I told her I had to catch up with one of the others from the recycling project. (I didn't – I just sat in the far-left cubicle of the Female Visitors' Toilets and drew doodles round my inner fairy at the back of this journal.)

So, yeah, I could come and help at Saturday's Big Bring-&-Swap Party. And though I might not be bringing my one and only friend, I'd probably be bringing a box of her ex-squirrels along. . .

"By the way, Rowan, don't take this the wrong way," Miss Boyle suddenly began, lowering her voice. It must have been so that Verity and Marlon – who were chatting and nibbling strands of hair (Verity, at least) – couldn't hear.

Uh-oh. What was Miss Boyle about to say?

My panic goblin did instant splits in my tummy. I'd had *quite* enough of things being taken the wrong way today already and my head was going *spinny* with it.

"But is everything OK with you? It's none of my business, but I was just a bit concerned that you've done such a U-turn with the way you dress and do your hair."

Urgh. You'd think I'd pierced my eyelids and come to school in a T-shirt that said *Kill All Teachers* instead of a hairband, regulation floppy fringe and sensible shoes.

"I'm fine!" I said with a throwaway laugh that probably sounded a little bit manic.

"Well, that's great," said Miss Boyle, putting her hand on mine, which made my eyes well up a bit, if you want to know the truth. "But I just want you to know that you're a very special, unique person, Rowan, and you don't *have* to be like everyone else if you don't feel comfortable that way."

"I feel comfortable *this* way," I said very quickly.

Mainly because being described as a special, unique person who doesn't have to be like everyone else makes me worry that I'm quite similar to one of those quiet, friendless blokes who turn out to be the axe murderer in horror movies.

(May have to rethink giving Miss Boyle Hero Crush status.)

Tuesday 9.48 p.m.
Right.

I'm trying not to think about – or stress over – friendships, OR Miss Boyle telling me I'm unique and special when all I want is to be boring and ordinary like Erin. (Didn't mean it *that* way. You *know* what I meant.)

Instead, like I decided, I finished copying out *all* the seventeen rules so far from this journal ultra-neatly in my delicious dark-pink pen.

Have finished for now and stuck the powder-pink sheet of Raspberry Rules over the daisy wallpaper rectangle, and they look very important and meaningful in the gold fancy frame!

Must go. Found one of those sticky pet-hair rollers in a drawer in the kitchen and should de-fluff some pants for school tomorrow.

Wednesday 7.41 a.m.

Woke up and realized it's only *five days* to Erin's birthday and I still have . . .

a) no idea what to get her; and
b) only £4.52 to get it with.

Other things I have woken up realizing:

1) When Erin spoke about worrying that people would see her squirrel collection, she was talking about Ingrid and Yaz, wasn't she?
2) When I called on Monday and spoke to her mum Gillian, Erin wasn't there because she was very probably hanging out with Ingrid and Yaz, right?
3) For her birthday ice-skate-and-burger trip, it's not just going to be me and *her*, is it? (Let me guess . . . Ingrid and Yaz might be invited too?)

I should ask Erin straight out about 1, 2 and 3.

But knowing my amazing lack of bravery, that's about as likely as Colin our three-legged cat learning the flamenco.

Wednesday 7.45 a.m.

Fluffy is sitting on the window sill looking longingly out at the garden, but is resisting all attempts to leave the safety of my room.

Oh, no . . . I think she might have agorophobia!!

Wednesday 8.15 a.m.

"<u>CATS</u> CAN'T GET AGOROPHOBIA!" Linn yelled at me over toast just now. "THINK ABOUT IT, RO; A HUGE DOG ONCE ATE HER TAIL! SHE PROBABLY THINKS *EVERY* ANIMAL WITH SHARP TEETH IS POTENTIALLY GOING TO BITE OFF ANOTHER BIT OF HER!!"

Linn is possibly right.

Wednesday 8.40 a.m.

Grandma arrived just a few minutes ago to take Tor to school.

Because she is quite a neat-freak person, I think she generally *approves* of my new look, though she keeps checking me out, as if she's worried that I've been swapped with an imposter alien from a very neat planet and I might swap back again unexpectedly.

The one thing she's not too keen on is the regulation floppy fringe practically everyone wears at school ("hmm, bit messy"). She couldn't help herself from leaning over to tidy it back off my face before I nipped upstairs for my bag just now.

"Rowan! What's happened to your forehead?" she asked, all concerned.

I was too embarrassed to tell her that I'd accidentally sandpapered it with the glitter on my (home-made) inner fairy, so I said something vague about it being a netball-related injury.

From the doubtful look in her eyes, I wasn't sure if Grandma was convinced or not, so I decided to quickly ramble on about other stuff to get her off the subject.

First, I rambled on about the Big Bring-&-Swap Party and told her she had to come.

Then I rambled on about how Georgie would be coming round today so we could work on a new, improved recycling idea.

Grandma said yes, *yes*, YES I'd told her a million times about both those facts, and she'd do pizza for tea.

(Must get her to show me how you make pizza, so I

can impress my family with it one weekend. I think it's the same recipe as fairy cakes, only with tomato sauce and cheese added on top.)

Wednesday 12.25 p.m.

NOOOOOOOO!!!!

I AM SUCH A *CHICKEN*!!!

Two seconds ago I came out of the far-left cubicle of the Female Visitors' Toilets, to find only ONE other person in there, hovering delicately and gorgeously in front of the mirrors. And who do you think that ONE person was?

Yep, she of the amazing crinkle-cut-chip hair, glittery green eyes and orange patent-leather shoes.

Libby-Mae Ferguson was fiddling with a pretty, multicoloured, beaded choker around her neck, and smelled of the lily of the valley hand wash that only the Female Visitors usually get spoiled with.

I *instantly* knew that I'd never get a better opportunity to talk to her.

And her fairy brooch was right here, pinned on the back of my blazer lapel, ready to give her the next time I saw her which was right that **EXACT** MOMENT!

But I made the fateful mistake of looking first at her reflection (beautiful, interesting, mesmerizing), and then fleetingly looking at mine (ordinary, uninteresting, panicked) and froze somewhere useless between the cubicles and the sinks.

"S'cuse!!" she said brightly, having to squeeze by me to leave.

She spoke and looked at the air above my head, as if I was the human equivalent of dust, only possibly less interesting.

Yep, I am a chicken, crossed with a dust molecule, and I *blew* it. . .

Wednesday 5.40 p.m.

I just walked along to Georgie's block of flats with her a little while ago (Rolf and Winslet needed their pre-tea walk).

Guess what she said to me, before she disappeared inside her building?

"Y'know, I was pretty *scared* of you."

I mean, *how* crazy is that? I'm about as scary as a sheep! (Or a chicken. . .)

"*When* were you scared of me?" I asked, remembering that glance she gave me by the Green Waste skip a week or so ago, like I was toxic.

"Uh, till about an hour ago."

!!!

It gets *madder*; apparently she was scared of me because she thought . . . wait for it . . . that I was super-cool.

!!!

HA, HA, HA!

Georgie said she only stopped being scared of me when I started singing along to the *Sound Of Music* video that was on in the background while we worked on recycling stuff. It was 'cause I sang out of tune, she said.

Do I sing out of tune?

I was *wondering* why she was giggling. . .

"Actually, I was sort of scared of *you* at first," I admitted right back to her. (You should have *seen* her eyebrows shoot up her forehead at that!)

"*Me?* Why?" she squeaked.

"Because you were quieter than a very shy black hole in deep space, so I thought you were mad at me AND 'cause you thought I was a freak or something."

"I didn't think you were a freak – I thought you were *amazing*, the way you used to dress!"

The way I <u>used</u> to dress . . . *that* was strange to hear. So that time I'd caught her staring at me by the giant skip; it was 'cause she *liked* what I was wearing, and *not* because she thought I was toxic?! Who'd've guessed!

"And anyway," Georgie carried on, "why would I have been *mad* at you?"

"Well, maybe 'cause I thought you were a *boy* at first. Though now I realize that's completely *insane*, since you're pretty and sort of have, er, *boobs*, obviously."

Did that sound clunky? I panicked, knowing that it absolutely did, and wishing my mouth would learn its lesson and wait for my brain to OK stuff first.

But it was all right. Straight away, Georgie said, "It's fine. People *always* reckon I'm a boy. It *used* to bother me, I guess till I met *you* and saw that you dressed how you wanted and didn't care what *anyone* thought."

Georgie gave me a shy smile, then waved and headed off into her block of flats, leaving me with two restless dogs and a major thought pinging around my head: I really, truly, never, *ever* bothered what people thought about the way I looked – till four days ago.

And that major thought made me feel a bit sorry and sad, really. Like I was homesick for my mad hair and stripy tights. . .

Or maybe that sorry, sad and homesick feeling was because I'd carried on looking normal and talked and talked and *talked* to Erin all day today, but didn't really feel like it was doing me any good at all.

The cooler she acted, the more I rambled. (It might be crazy, but I felt like every second I was with her, she was wondering where Ingrid and Yaz were.)

Y'know, I'd spent the whole day with my panic goblin break-dancing in my chest and it had been a real relief to come home and hang out with Georgie — even if we'd come up with precisely *no* project ideas at all. Oops.

And oops again — I'm sort of telling this whole day slightly back-to-front, aren't I? (Probably because my head feels like it's on back-to-front.)

Never mind.

The good news is that me and Georgie did at least sew a whole *bunch* of Marlon and Yusuf's Bag Bags. Miss Boyle had handed me, William, Marlon and Verity a batch of material each today and ordered us (with a big smile) to get on with stitching them together over the next few days so we can screen-print them on Monday when we all get together.

There was *one* weeny snag when Georgie first turned up at my house earlier, though. . .

"I can't sew," she'd muttered worriedly, gazing down at the material and the needle and thread laid out on our coffee table. It was as if I'd asked her to dissect a frog.

Immediately, I put my teacher hat on and gave her a

lesson – she picked it up super-quick – and while we hand-stitched and ate biscuits, I stuck on *The Sound Of Music*, since it is the best movie in the world (in my opinion). Also, I thought Georgie might like it, seeing as it's historical and set in Austria during the war and stuff (as well as having singing nuns* and kids in it).

By the time Georgie left, we had made nineteen Bag Bags, all ready for screen-printing.

It *would* have been twenty, but one dropped on the floor and Winslet ran off with it.

---

* I have a Hero Crush on Julie Andrews, who plays Maria, the main singing nun in the film. It's because she's been in a couple more of my favourite movies like *Mary Poppins* and *The Princess Diaries*. I once tried to write to her when I was Tor's age, but she didn't write back, possibly because she was very busy, or possibly because I addressed it to

Maria
The Hills That Are Alive
Sound of Music
Austria

Wednesday 8.23 p.m.

Who knew a snack could give me inspiration for a present?

Maybe it was the peanut butter; after all, it's full of protein, and protein is good for your BRAIN.

Anyway, the peanut butter jar was empty, and I was

twiddling the lid round in my fingers, wondering what I could give Erin that would . . .

a) mean something,
b) remind her of our friendship, and
c) not cost more than £4.52.

And then it came to me!

I scrabbled around in my drawers and boxes (and around an intrigued Fluffy) till I got all the exact right stuff, i.e.:

- A bit of my daisy wallpaper as a background, torn from the unpainted rectangle behind my bed (represents all the happy times we hung out in my room).
- A giggly photo booth pic of us taken last year (our eyes are closed, but it's still pretty funny).
- A tiny white shell from the time her parents took us to Southend beach for the day (we ate candyfloss the size of our heads).
- The key to the secret diary we started writing together in Year Seven (though we lost the diary in the park).
- The cutest and tiniest of her squirrel collection

(represents all the happy times we hung out in HER room).

Yes!!

Will glue it all together and add a sprinkle of purple glitter, since purple is Erin's favourite colour.

It'll be so cute and so personal and so *us* that she won't be able not to love it!

{ CRAFT INSTRUCTIONS }

Mini memory shrine
You'll need:
- An empty jar or tin lid
- Strong glue
- Precious bits and bobs, like cute mini toys and shells
- Glitter or ribbon

Instructions:
1) Make sure your lid is clean and dry (i.e., don't just lick it clean of strawberry jam or whatever).
2) Choose lots of bits and bobs that will fit in and look good together.

3) Glue them in with strong glue.
4) Do finishing touches with glitter or ribbon wrapped round the edge.
5) Present your mini memory shrine to someone who will say "Awww!!"

Thursday 7.45 a.m.

Erin will HATE it.

What was I *thinking*?

Why would she love something with one of her old squirrel things stuck on it? Didn't she chuck them all away?

What am I going to do?

What am I going to buy her for a present?

I feel like feeding the stupid mini shrine to Winslet right *now*. . .

Thursday 5.15 p.m.

"*Do you have any queries?*" it said. . .

Y'know, I have just done something slightly nuts.

Oh, and I've told a slight lie.

The lie part was asking Miss Whyte the librarian for permission to send an email query to a website which was connected to the recycling project I was doing with Miss Boyle. (It wasn't.)

The nuts part was . . . well, I'll come to that in a minute.

It all came about because I couldn't find Erin at break time this morning.

And then, as I was wandering along the main corridor, I saw Ingrid and Yaz, so I asked, "Have you seen Erin?" and they swapped little glances with each other and both said, "No," which translated in my paranoid ears as "*Yes*, but you're WAY weird and we're not saying where we've seen her."

Then in class, Erin sounded all grumpy when I asked where she'd been and muttered about how she'd only gone off to check out the old loos now they've been repaired and – hey! – we weren't Vietnamese twins joined at the *hip* or anything.

Even though I knew Erin'd got it wrong and meant *Siamese* (the old name for conjoined twins), she made me feel *completely* stupid and clingy with that one mutter.

So I decided I'd better give her LOTS of space and skipped lunch, even though it was spaghetti bolognese day in the dining hall. (Though it meant I had to spend £1.45 on a bottle of water and a cereal bar so I wouldn't get malnutrition.)

At first, I hung out in the far-left-hand cubicle of the Female Visitors' Toilets and tried doodling some relaxing stars around my inner fairy at the back of this journal, but it didn't make me feel any better.

So I wandered here to the library and looked up the Find Your Inner Fairy website, in the hope that looking at incredible handmade fairy wings might cheer me up.

And then I saw it: just those few little words.

"*Do you have any queries?*"

"*Yes, I have a query!*" I keyed into the email box, as soon as super-website-safety-concious Miss Whyte gave me the OK to email out a research-based question (sorry, sorry, sorry for lying, Miss Whyte!).

And here's what I sent. . .

"*What do you do when your best friend doesn't want to be your best friend any more? Love from Rowan Love xxx*"

Now I'll just have to keep my fingers crossed for a reply that can make me feel better.

Specially since the query box was really just about ordering tutus. . .

Thursday 11.35 p.m.
Can't sleep for guilt.

I'm not very comfortable about lying, and I lied to

Miss Whyte about why I needed to email, and that is BIG-TIME bad because:

a) we've had it drummed into us a million times in ICT class that you never, ever wantonly give out your personal details online in case exceptionally weirdy people get hold of your info, and
b) Miss Whyte was so kind that she gave her own personal pudding to me that time my scarf strangled me, which makes me guilty AND ungrateful.

Thursday 11.55 p.m.

Aaargh!

Must have fallen asleep, but had a guilt-induced nightmare that a weirdy face was *loooooming* out of a computer at me, and I couldn't breathe.

!!!

Then woke up and realized Fluffy was sitting on my chest staring straight at me.

I have learned three things from this:

- I must never lie to nice, trusting librarians again.
- I must never give out details willy-nilly online again.
- Fluffy really, *really* needs more friends than just me. . .

FRIDAY

Friday 7.38 a.m.

Wow, it's exhausting being normal.

I nearly forgot this morning and automatically reached for my sweetie hair clips.

But no; I've got to *stick* with what I've started, which means blow-drying my floppy fringe (to a perfect state of floppiness), resisting all jewellery (requires mega will power) and hoping that my one pair of plain black tights are dry after I washed them last night (they were a bit damp when I grabbed them off the radiator and put them on yesterday – yuck!).

I'm also exhausted because I had *another* nightmare last night and couldn't get back to sleep for *ages**.

In *this* dream, I was being chased down a street I didn't know by something *bad* that I couldn't see, and I was completely naked apart from the squirrel knickers I made for Erin.

If that's not terrifically weird, I don't know what is.

* Took my pillow and duvet down beside the bottom drawer of my wardrobe, where my jumpers are, so that Fluffy's purring could soothe me to sleep. I've relocated her there from my pants drawer, as it's quite warm weather just now and I won't have to worry about excessively hairy jumpers till winter. Fluffy wasn't too thrilled with the move, so I had to put a couple of my oldest pairs of pants in there (like the Little Miss Chatterbox, age nine, ones) to make her feel at home.

Friday 8.59 a.m.
I'm in my office. Ha, ha, ha!

I don't think we're meant to be using the Female Visitors' Toilets any more now that the regular girls' loos downstairs have been mended, but nobody's said that for sure, so until they do, I'm going to carry on using these ones 'cause of their higher standard of décor (the fake flower arrangements, not the graffiti) and hand wash.

By the way, Grandma spotted me yawning my head off this morning and asked what was up. I told her about my dream, and she said, "That is a *classic* anxiety dream."

I was a bit confused; I thought she meant worried people regularly dream about squirrel knickers, but then she explained that the classic part was dreaming about being outside naked or in your pyjamas or something equally stupid and embarrassing.

Anyway, Grandma said, "Is there something making you feel anxious at the moment, Rowan?" and I panicked a bit then, because me and Linn and Ally sort of have this unwritten rule* that we don't tell Dad or Grandma about stuff that is making us stressed. It's 'cause – like I've said before – we know they're both pretty sensitive about Mum not being around if one of us happens to be feeling wobbly.

(Y'know, I wish they wouldn't think like that, 'cause although we miss Mum tons and people are weirded out by her being away, I *do* get a kick from boasting about the latest exotic country we've had postcards from. It sure beats saying your mum's at the supermarket and is addicted to soaps or something.)

So anyway, I told Grandma a true fact: that I was worried about what to get Erin for her birthday, although what was TRUER was that I was worried I wasn't going to have Erin as a best friend for very much longer. . .

Grandma crossed her arms and looked thoughtful for a second. "Well, why don't you get her a top? I'm sure you know what she likes!" she suggested.

Of *course* I knew what Erin liked. The problem was

that the T-shirts and tops she'd go for would cost more than £3.07. (I think I'll only be able to afford a card and wrapping paper for £3.07, if I'm lucky.)

Maybe Grandma was a bit psychic, 'cause then she said, "Do you have enough money, Rowan?"

I lied and said yes, because I didn't want her to think I'd been stupid and bought useless stuff like liquid eyeliner (which I'd used up sleep-writing on my wall), cheap ballet pumps (ruined and dumped) and yellow sparkly eyeshadow (eaten).

But like I say, I think my super-sensible grandma might be able to read minds, because she laughed and then gave me a big hug.

Oh, and she's a magician too, because when the hug ended, I found a ten-pound note in my hand.

(I do love my grandma.)

* Can't exactly write *that* on my Raspberry Rules list, since it would be a bit of a giveaway next time Dad or Grandma wandered into my room.

Friday 12.40 p.m.
I GOT A REPLY TO MY EMAIL!!! EEEEEEEEKKK!!!
!!!

(As I read it, I felt a huge tidal wave of guilt and ungratefulness wash over me, and sat about three centimetres from the screen so that any passing, trusting librarians couldn't see what was on screen.)

It said. . .

> *Dear Customer,*
> *Thank you for your email.*
> *Unfortunately, this address is only for ordering*
> *fairy wings, wands and tutus, etc., and we can't*
> *answer personal mail.*
> *All the best,*
> *Sacha Fairy (Customer Services)*
> *"May a sprinkle of fairy dust waft your way*
> *with this email"*

Wow, wow, WOW!!!

I'm so excited and happy I could *cry*.

OK, so Sacha* Fairy couldn't help me, but isn't that sweet? The part about the fairy dust?!

Hey, maybe the fairy dust is here already!!!

* Rowan Sacha Love . . . Rowan Sacha *Fairy* Love. . .? Would having "Fairy" as a middle name be cute, or mad? Or both?)

Friday 2.39 p.m.
Don't think the fairy dust has arrived.

Sure, Erin has been talking to me today, but just to say "Can you pass the protractor?" and "Have you done Mr Jong's homework yet?" and "No, I can't come to the Big Bring-&-Swap Party tomorrow because I'm going shopping with Mum."

It's very hard to think fluffy thoughts when your best friend is just saying bland, non-best-friend stuff like that.

And it's practically *impossible* to feel fluffy when Ingrid stops your best friend in the corridor between classes like just now and says, "So what time will me and Yaz meet you up at the ice rink on Sunday?" and makes you realize that you were right about a certain extra two someones being invited along to your best friend's birthday treat. . .

"You never said Ingrid and Yaz were coming too," I tried to say in a cheerful and unclingy voice when we went into class. It came out a bit wobbly.

"Oh, I thought I did," Erin fibbed, which felt not very fantastic.

In fact, I felt SO not-fantastic that I pretended to Mr Svenson that I needed a wee and got a pass to come out here to the Female Visitors' Toilets.

I'm so depressed that I just turned to the back of this journal and drew a beard and glasses on my inner fairy.

Friday 8.30 p.m.

Ooh, I've had a really cosy time on the sofa, just me and Dad (and Rolf, Derek and Colin).

Tor went to bed at 6.45 p.m. – his class had a trip to London Zoo today and he was so phenomenally excited that his brain imploded with happiness, I think.

Linn is at her mate Alfie's house, and Ally went round to Sandie's for tea.

It's not very often that any of us get Dad to ourselves, and it was lovely tonight, 'cause Dad and me made popcorn after Tor snoozed off and talked about lots of random stuff, like what colour he wants to paint his peeling shop sign (pity there's no more Ra-Ra-Raspberry!) and what we should do about making Fluffy feel like less of an outsider (wish pets liked parties – it usually works to get people talking).

Then for some reason Dad took out all our old photo albums to look at.

It was fun seeing pictures of Mum and of us at all different sizes, weeny to *BIG*.

He asked me what my favourite was, and I chose the school photo of Linn when she was seven, because she is doing something very, *very* unusual in it, i.e., *smiling*.

I also like it because her teeth look *crazy*; there are

tiddly baby teeth that haven't fallen out yet and gaps where some have, and *ginormous* new teeth that look like she's borrowed them from a very big man, which is pretty funny. (Linn once said she was going to "RIP THAT STUPID PHOTO UP!!!" one of these days.)

Dad said, "Hey, here's *my* favourite!", and – get this! – it was of *ME*!!!

It was on my third birthday, and even though Mum had bought me a new dress, I'd wanted to choose my own special outfit, which is why I'm wearing a spotty swimsuit, a ballet skirt, a nurse's hat and wings made out of cardboard and tinfoil to my party.

"You can't really see your feet there, but you'd glued a whole packet of gift-wrap rosettes to your wellies," Dad reminisced. "Ahhh! Your mum always *did* say you had a bit of sparkle to you. . ."

Then he gave me a *huge* squashy hug and it was extra-specially wonderful till Rolf, our dopey dog, lunged bodily at the bowl of popcorn, slid off the coffee table and temporarily knocked himself out by headbutting the TV.

Friday 9.01 p.m.
Rolf's fine. He's now chasing his tail.

Friday 9.03 p.m.

Or *is* he fine? Maybe it's a sign of concussion!

Well, if he's got concussion, he's sure making it look like a *lot* of fun.

SATURDAY

Saturday 9.25 a.m.

Interesting post today!

We got a letter from Mum; our first for weeks! She is in Guatemala, which is near Russia, I think (must have a look at the giant map of the world in Ally's room and check). She has been working in a café and has saved enough money to travel to Namibia (Poland?).

But apart from Mum's lovely letter, I got (wait for it!) a parcel . . . yep, I won another COMPETITION!!! Can you believe it?!

The trouble is (and don't want to sound ungrateful), it's the tube of Mosiguard mosquito spray plus two car-window sun shields.

As my family doesn't have enough money for a car OR holidays where mosquitos live, I've decided to take them along to the Big Bring-&-Swap Party this afternoon. I will also be taking the box of small squirrelly things that Erin dumped. Sir Timothy Nutkins is sticking around, though, as Tor said Mr Penguin has specifically requested that he stay.

Speaking of Tor, this morning he stared at me for the longest time while I blow-dried my fringe floppy and then muttered, "I liked you better when you were you."

???

By the way, I found Grandma's *Hornsey Journal* from Friday (lining the bottom of the hamster cage) and have entered competitions to win the following stuff:

- A packet of Duracell AA batteries
- A dictionary of rhyming slang
- A humidifier (???)
- "Blast It!" slug pellets (accidentally entered for that in a rush — will have to hide them from Tor if I win them)

Anyway, I'm still holding out for the laptop from the last edition. Wouldn't it be great to be able to look at the Find Your Inner Fairy website at home? (Though I wouldn't write to them again. I have learned my lesson. I realize that I was very lucky this time that the person who got back to me was a customer services fairy who couldn't help me, rather than a weirdy bloke who'd use my email address to send dodgy spam or try and arrange a date with me in a grotty transport café on the M40.)

Saturday 11.49 a.m.

I'm just back from H&M in Wood Green. With Grandma's money I bought Erin a skinny-fit dark blue long-sleeved T-shirt for £6.99. It's kind of boring. She'll love it.

There was another one in grey; maybe I should have got that too? There *was* an offer on for two T-shirts for £12. I could've worn it to the ice rink tomorrow.

But then IF I'd bought it, I wouldn't have been able to afford a card and wrapping paper, and I don't suppose Erin would appreciate getting a present wrapped in the property section of the *Hornsey Journal*.

Saturday 4.05 p.m.

Hurray for the Big Bring-&-Swap Party!

I'm just sitting waiting for Miss Boyle to find some bin bags so we can tidy up the stuff that's left.

Everyone else from Miss Boyle's group is in the café (i.e., the Alexandra Hill School staffroom) eating the fairy cakes that didn't get sold today. But after all the noise and chaos this afternoon, I thought it'd be nice to sit here and be quiet and do my journal for a few minutes.

(Oh, I WISH I hadn't drawn the beard and glasses on my inner fairy. . .).

Anyway, about the Big Bring-&-Swap Party; it went brilliantly! For two hours there was this BIG scrum of people dumping stuff on the tables that me, Miss Boyle, everyone on our project and some of the Alexandra Hill teachers had laid out, and then *blam!*, they were all scrabbling around and grabbing a whole bunch of *other* stuff to take home again.

Practically *everything* went except . . .

1) a plastic bag full of scruffy-looking socks (yew!!),
2) a man's white shirt with yellow sweat stains under the armpits (yew!! yew!!),
3) a guitar with no strings or neck (mmm, useful!),
4) a very thick, dog-eared book called *Commercial Law and Accountancy* (zzz. . .),
5) a Nike trainer, size 13 (yep, just one!), and
6) heaps and *heaps* of junky bits of small plastic toys (like all the useless stuff kids get in party bags).

Oh, and 7) the squirrel collection, 'cause *somehow* the

box it was in accidentally ended up tucked under a chair against the wall. I think it was when Omar and Yusuf were having a race; Omar was grinning away as he *boinged* on a pogo stick, and Yusuf was stony-faced in concentration on a semi-deflated Space Hopper.

Speaking of high-speed stupidness, at one point William squashed himself into a kids' pedal car that got donated and told us all to call him Jenson Button, after the famous Formula Whatever racing driver. He said if anyone dared to forget, there would be serious consequences; i.e., he'd run over their feet.

Verity forgot.

She started nervously eating her hair as ~~William~~ Jenson Button stared at her and pretended to rev up, which is when Miss Boyle ordered him outside into the playground.

He made *straight* for Verity on his way, but she stopped eating her hair long enough to leap on to an unwanted plastic garden chair. So William had to make do with scooping up a nearby Bianca instead (very easy, as she weighs about as much as a packet of biscuits) and giving her very fast rides down the dining hall ramp on the car bonnet till the Alexandra Hill head teacher ordered him to stop on the grounds of health and safety – as well as noise pollution (Bianca was doing a lot of screaming, apparently).

But back to the Big Bring-&-Swap Party.

There were lots of school parents milling around, and our group had done a pretty good job of inviting people along; for me, it was Grandma, Tor and Ally (Dad works Saturdays, and Linn has a phobia about untidiness and anything second-hand, so I knew she wouldn't exactly be at the head of the queue to come in).

It wasn't just *me*, of course; there was always a mum or granny or a friend yoo-hoo-ing or yo!-ing every five minutes at Verity or Marlon or Jenson Button or our buddies.

Marlon was brilliant, by the way, when quite a *weird* thing happened with Georgie's mum.

Me, him, Bianca and Georgie were all working on the same stretch of tables (which meant scooping stuff up when overenthusiastic rummaging sent it flopping to the floor). Georgie's little pink, frilly sisters were hovering around the buggy nearby, eating their Wotsits nicely, while Georgie's big pink, frilly mum held some super-tight cropped jeans up against her.

OK, so the truth was, those jeans looked more like they'd fit Bianca than Georgie's mum. But that didn't make it right that these two lads about our age started laughing and making *pig* noises right behind her, for goodness' sake.

!!!

Luckily, Georgie's mum didn't seem to notice. *Georgie* did, though; that was pretty obvious to me and Marlon and Bianca.

I spotted that Georgie was clenching her fists, and looked like she was wavering between wanting to either *punch* the boys or cry.

"Do you know them?" Marlon muttered to her.

He's very cool. He has this laid-back expression that doesn't ever give much away.

"They're Cameron and Karl. They're in my class," Georgie muttered back through thin, tight lips. "They *always* do this stuff!"

"What stuff?" I asked her quietly, pretty sure what she meant. If I had hackles, I'd feel them rising.

"Go on about my mum," Georgie whispered back bleakly.

"They laugh at me too. Guess *why*. . ." Bianca added just as bleakly, her pretty face thunderous.

Ooh, this was Fluffy and the Rottweiler all over again. Same as a monster-sized dog turning on an animal that was no bigger than its *head*, it was just so, so easy to be two cocky lads ganging up on one shy girl and one tiny girl, wasn't it?

I felt absolutely furious, but I didn't know what to do.

Luckily, *Marlon* did.

He ducked under the table and came up right by the boys, and just glared *eerily* at them, for what felt like for ever.

"Yeah, *what*?" said Cameron/Karl (didn't know which was which, and instantly didn't want to know them well enough to tell the difference).

Marlon said nothing, and kept right on silently staring at them. If I'd been on the other end of that stare, I would've been totally intimidated. Actually, I *wasn't* on the end of that stare, and I was *well* intimidated.

Cameron/Karl and Karl/Cameron were starting to look uncomfortable.

In the circumstances, they did the only thing they could; they pretended to laugh (sounded nervous) and mooched awkwardly off.

"Marlon, that was *amazing*!!" Georgie muttered, once her mum and sisters had wandered off to the tearoom in search of fairy cakes.

Bianca nodded madly, staring up in awe of Marlon and his amazing death-ray stare.

Marlon did this "Yeah, whatever" shrug. But somehow I did suddenly think about him being expelled from his last school.

If I ever get brave enough*, I'll have to ask him about the whole supergluing-the-head-teacher's-door-shut thing**.

* Yep, I'll never be brave enough.
** So I'll never ask him.

Saturday 4.25 p.m.

Miss Boyle came out into the hall a few minutes ago with bin bags, and while we started to fill them, we had this really nice conversation!

She asked if I'd had some of the leftover fairy cakes, and I said I wasn't hungry, and then showed her my journal (well, not the stuff *inside*). Next Miss Boyle told me that *she'd* kept a diary when she was thirteen, till her older brother went and read what she'd said about him (that his acne made his face look like a pizza with chicken pox) and he tore out all the pages and flushed them down the loo.

Finally she made this very intuitive and perceptive comment (good use of vocabulary; tick!).

"Are you all right, at the moment, Rowan? I mean, I

know there was that business with the graffiti, but I have a feeling something *else* is bothering you. . ."

Now maybe it's because I'm so used to NOT telling Dad and Grandma what's *really* bothering me, but I immediately launched into talking about a Lower Level Worry than losing my best friend.

"Well, me and Georgie just haven't really managed to think of a project," I said, sweeping my arm around to show the difference between the mega-successful jumble non-sale, and our non-project.

"But you've done brilliantly, Rowan!" she answered me back. "You came up with the name for today's event, you and Georgie have sewn a pile of Bag Bags, and you've helped William and Omar hand out all their leaflets today. That sounds very good to me!"

It was sweet of her to say so. And then she added, "But is that *all*? Or is there anything else on your mind?"

The way she gazed all kindly and concerned, tilting her head over cutely like a little round robin, it was as if she already *knew*.

And because she wasn't Dad or Grandma, I just came out with it: The Real Problem. I mean, about how Ingrid and Yaz were stealing Erin away, and how I'd been trying my best to be a better friend, i.e., one who was non-annoying, either in person or the way I dressed.

"The thing is, Rowan," Miss Boyle began once I'd finished blurting, "I don't think you *should* change. Maybe—"

I don't know what else she was planning on saying, because right then *everyone* bundled out of the café/staffroom. They started grabbing bin bags and madly scooping up mostly fiddly little *useless* chunks of coloured plastic toys. After a frantic blur of tidying, the bags were loaded into Miss Boyle's car to take to the dump on Monday.

I'm now sitting out on the grass in Ally Pally park, eating a fairy cake that Miss Boyle shoved in my hand before she drove off.

The rest of our group has gone home already.

("Want to hang out for a while?" I asked Georgie, but her bright-pink family were waiting outside for her by the school gates.)

That's OK, though – I'm pretty much enjoying sitting here on my own in the sunshine, just mulling over what Miss Boyle said.

Oh, and I'm also staring up at the palace where the ice rink is, and sort of wondering how tomorrow's birthday do is going to go.

I'm also hoping that that Staffie in the distance isn't running towards me and my fairy cake. . .

Saturday 8.45 p.m.

Fluffy *still* isn't getting on brilliantly with the other pets. (Colin hopped into my room earlier and Fluffy hissed so madly at him that she lost her voice/hiss.)

Forget agorophobia and Rottweiller stress; Tor has THIS theory about Fluffy . . . that her hissy fits and unfriendliness have got something to do with her having no tail.

Maybe she's self-conscious? Or maybe our dogs and other cats are confused and think she's a giant guinea pig?

So after tea, I decided to *knit* her a tail.

I unravelled my snipped-up skinny scarf and knitted this vaguely tail-shaped, er, *shape*, then sewed it to a bit of red ribbon, which I then tied round her tummy.

At first, she lay on the rug in the middle of my bedroom floor purring, so I thought she quite liked it. (I took a photo.) Then she started to give her woolly "tail" the evil eye, and tore it to shreds. (Pretty funny – I took another photo.)

But, y'know, while I was making the tail and then watching Fluffy kill it, all these random thoughts started rambling around in my mind.

. . .Verity asking me what had happened to my sweetie hair clips earlier when we were setting up for the Big Bring-&-Swap Party. . .

. . .Georgie thinking I was super-cool (ha!) when she first met me. . .

. . .Dad's favourite photo of me in my tinfoil wings and gift-wrap rosette wellies. . .

. . .Tor saying he liked me better when I was me. . .

. . .Miss Boyle saying maybe I shouldn't change. . .

. . .Sacha Fairy sending me fairy dust in her email. . .

All that inner-head rambling put together has suddenly – BLAM!! (actually, it was more of a FIZZZZ!!) – made me decide two things:

1) I'm going to take this pair of scissors I just snipped the red ribbon with and cut my plain black tights into tiny, weeny pieces, and . . .

2) one way or another, I'm DESTINED to go to next Saturday's Fairy Fun Day in Trafalgar Square.

'Cause the thing is, I really, *really* miss being <u>ME</u>.

!!!

SUNDAY

Sunday 305 p.m.

People have this idea that ice-skating is all graceful and everything, but you just have to watch some of the shows on TV to see that celebs and anyone else having a go are always breaking bits of themselves.

Also, it is *freezing*.

So last night and this morning, I put together a graceful but safe and practical outfit for Erin's ice-skating birthday do today.

It consists of:

- my stripy white, blue and mauve woolly tights and Dad's white Aran jumper (the practical bit),
- a bicycle helmet (the safe part),
- some old white lace net curtains from the loft (the graceful part).

I only meant to sew some short panels of net curtain on to a pair of white knickers to make myself a cute little skating tutu. But then I thought it would be kind of fun to attach a really *long* piece of netting to the *back* of the tutu – like the train of a wedding dress, or an angel's dress flying over the Himalayas! – so it would swoosh all elegantly behind me when I sped around the ice.

After the success of my skirt, the Barbie crash helmet looked kind of *wrong* next to it, so I sewed a leftover bit of net curtain over it to cover up all the brightly coloured Barbie-ness.

And *voila*, I had my complete outfit.

But then *ping!*, an extra twinkle of inspiration fluttered into my head; there was this dusty bunch of white fabric roses stuck in a flower bed in the garden, marking the spot where we buried one of Tor's goldfish last month. I got it in my head that they might look great sewn as a bustle at the back of my train, and maybe woven through the holes in my helmet to match. (Tor was cool. I said I'd help him paint a sign that said *"Boris, swimming with the angels, RIP"* in their place.)

"Wow, Rowan! You're just like the White Witch out of *The Chronicles of Narnia!*" said Erin's mum Gillian, when I wandered into the ice-rink reception to meet everyone.

"Your Majesty!" said Erin's dad Dave, dropping down into this theatrical bow.

On his way back up, he grabbed my hand, kissed the back of it, and did this waffle welcoming me to my "snowy kingdom".

I think Erin's parents were going over the top with the enthusiasm 'cause *they* knew and *I* knew that the last time we'd seen each other, I was disappearing into some bushes outside of the circus.

But anyway, even if they *were* just trying to cover up for any embarrassment, the stuff they were saying was pretty funny.

Well, obviously not to Erin, Ingrid and Yaz. They all stared at me from under their identikit floppy fringes like I'd turned up smeared in Marmite.

But I didn't care.

I just felt so OVER being normal.

I'd done it for a whole week, and being normal had felt as, well . . . as normal to me as a snail mooing. Thing is, I decided last night that Erin was just going to have to like me for who I was, or . . . well, I didn't want to think about the "or" bit.

So what happened?

Picture the scene: Erin opened her present (the long-sleeved T-shirt) and loved it. We all sang happy birthday. Then me, Erin, Ingrid and Yaz put our skates on and whizzed around the ice, having a ball. At one point, Erin came alongside me and grabbed my hand, giving it a squeeze, and we skated faster and faster, grinning at each other and laughing, knowing without saying anything that we'd come through this strange little phase in our friendship and it was all going to be OK; i.e., happy ever after from now on.

Oops! That's not *quite* how it went.

Erin liked her present for sure, but the other stuff...

Let's see; somehow Erin and Ingrid and Yaz kept skating *just* ahead of me, never slowing to let me catch up.

Erin didn't glance back, as if she'd forgotten I was even there, though I spotted Ingrid and Yaz checking me out over their shoulders a couple of times.

I saw Erin's dad Dave and her mum Gillian watching us all – they gave me huge waves and thumbs up whenever I whizzed by them. Did they see what was happening? That I was ever-so-unsubtly being frozen out?

My panic goblin was spinning around in my chest, doing his own fancy spins and jumps.

I felt like packing it in, gathering up my train and

going home. Then this old track I love came on the sound system – "Freak Like Me" by the Sugababes – and I thought, why not pretend I'm here on my own, and just zoom, *zoom*, ZOOM around for the next few minutes?

So I zoom, *zoom*, ZOOMED, and then did this BIG twirl . . .

. . . and ended up tangling some little kid on a skating lesson in my train, so that me and him and his instructor ended up in a big pile of netting and bruises and blades.

"*God, Rowan!!*"

I saw Erin glower down at me.

Another time, my best friend might have helped me up, instead of slapping me down with two words in front of the whole of the ice rink. Maybe she should have asked to use the speaker, to make sure no one missed how embarrassed and annoyed she was by me.

"Just *leave* her to it. . ." I heard Ingrid say, turning away from me and pulling at Erin's arm.

And *that's* when I lost it.

"Why don't *you* and *Yaz* just leave instead?" I blurted, fury and unfairness making me temporarily brave. (Though I was glad I was sprawled flat on my back on the ice — I'd have given away my natural cowardliness by shaking if I'd been standing. Though the kid trying to untangle his legs from mine probably felt me go all trembly.)

Ingrid and Yaz stared down at me as if I was a scrunched-up piece of litter in the gutter.

Arrgh . . . that look only made me *more* furious, and made me blurt out something ELSE that had been bugging me.

"What are you waiting for? Haven't you two got toilet doors you want to write nasty graffiti on?"

"*What?!*" barked Yaz, staring down at me. "What are you *on* about?"

I couldn't answer. I just felt hurt (my feelings, my left wrist and my bum).

It might be very easy to leave a normal party with your dignity intact. It's just that it's very tricky to leave an ice-skating party when you . . .

a) are attached to a small boy by a length of netting,
b) have accidentally turned into the whole ice rink's entertainment for the afternoon,
c) can't get up on your skates, and . . .
d) have a hand that hurts so much that it's agony

trying to undo your laces so you can escape.

By the way, I'm writing this in the waiting room at the Whittington Hospital.

Erin's dad Dave is off trying to phone home to let *my* dad and everyone know that I just *might* have a fractured wrist.

Erin is probably sitting in the posh burger restaurant in Muswell Hill with Ingrid and Yaz, celebrating the official end of our friendship.

Wonder when the fairy dust's meant to arrive?

WEEK 4

MONDAY

Monday 7.59 a.m.
Is it possible to have two *wildly* opposite feelings going on at the same time?

Because I do.

Right now, I feel brilliant AND awful.

I feel <u>AWFUL</u> because . . .

a) my wrist is hurting like crazy, and . . .

b) I am best-friend-less (Raspberry Rule No. 18: *I will get myself a NEW best friend – preferably one who isn't easily annoyed or embarrassed**).

And I feel <u>BRILLIANT</u> because . . .

. . . I had the most inspirational secret sleepwalking session last night!

It started when I had the squirrel pants dream (again). Only *this* time – while I was being chased semi-naked down a street I didn't know by something *bad* that I couldn't see – I spotted Fluffy's tailless, furry bum turn a corner *just* ahead of me.

I shot after her, and *blam!*, right up ahead on this *new* street was the most *amazing* view of a rainbow filling the ENTIRE sky, made of different colours of *rubbish*!!

There were green glass bottles and blue dishwasher-tablet-carton lids and yellow banana skins, and other stuff that I didn't get a chance to work out because I woke up suddenly and found myself on my knees, staring at a cloud-filled sky.

OK, so it was actually Ally's cloud-patterned duvet cover.

"Are you all right, Ro?" she asked, squinting at me sleepily like a meerkat peeking out of a burrow. (If meerkats *have* burrows. I'm not sure.)

Yep, I'd managed to wander upstairs and into my sister's attic bedroom while completely asleep.

"Just came to borrow a . . ." I looked around her room quickly for an alibi ". . . a shoelace!"

Ally seemed fine with that, and started snoozling again. (Luckily, she hadn't noticed it was 5.45 a.m.)

Still, as I was awake so early, it gave me plenty of time to sort out my outfit. And so today's school uniform is accessorized with ... *drum roll, please* ...

- pink nail varnish (dark pink and light pink alternating),
- crinkle-cut-chip hair (Ally did my plaits all neatly for me last night), clipped up at the side with sweetie butterfly hair clips (dark pink, from strips of a sheeny-shiny Turkish Delight wrapper),
- a choker made from pink beads and a white shoelace,
- sparkly pink eyeshadow (well, lipgloss, technically, as I don't have pink eyeshadow),
- my black flip-flops with pink ribbon bows (Mrs Wells might complain, but I'll just wave my wrist for sympathy),
- my pink plaster cast (who knew they did them in such cute different colours?).

And yes, it feels BRILLIANT to be dressed like this again.

Y'know what Tor yelled when I went down for breakfast just now?

"Yay! It's *you*!!", like I'd been away on a trip or something for a week.

I guess I have, in a way. I went to Normal-Land and

I didn't like it much. I'm very, *very* glad to be home.

Everyone in my family was super-kind to me when I got home from the hospital yesterday, by the way. Even Linn (!!) who made me macaroni cheese with one dollop of mustard and two dollops of tomato ketchup, which is *exactly* how I like it.

Dad stuck on our ancient video of *The Sound of Music* and then sat on the sofa with his arm around me, all snuggly.

Ally detached Fluffy from the pants in my drawer (she's defected back from the jumpers) and brought her down to sit on my lap. (Nice gesture, but she ran straight upstairs again.)

Tor got Graham the Snail Take Two to slither up and down my plaster cast and leave some attractive silvery lines (he used a buttercup as bait).

And get this; in the face of all this family friendliness, I crumbled. I mean, I blabbed *everything* about what had happened; the whole messy friendship disaster.

"Oh, Rowan, honey, don't cry," Dad had said, giving me a hug, since I had tears and watery snot streaming attractively down my face at the time. "Maybe you and Erin need time apart to appreciate each other."

Nice try, but I didn't really think *that* was going to happen. Neither did Linn, obviously. "FORGET ABOUT

ERIN, RO! SOUNDS LIKE SHE'S BEEN TRYING TO FORGET ABOUT *YOU*!!"

It seemed like good advice, but it's really quite hard to forget someone who sits next to you in *every* class. . .

* Slight problem: I wrote out my Raspberry Rules (1–17) very neatly. *So* neatly that I haven't left room for any more. Oops! Will go and squeeze No. 18 in at the bottom now. It's just about do-able if I use teeny-weeny doll-size writing. . .

Monday 10:45 a.m.

I'm in my ensuite office (ha ha ha).

And here's an interesting question:

Was sitting next to Erin this morning . . .

1) uncomfortable?
2) weird?
3) weirdly OK?

And the answer is: all three!!!

Erin was actually quite sweet – sweeter to me than she's been in ages!

I get the feeling that maybe her parents have pointed out to her that she hasn't been particularly fair or kind or nice to me in the last couple of weeks. Well, it's not *just* a feeling; on the way to the hospital yesterday, Erin's dad Dave told me, "We've been a bit disappointed by the way our Erin's been treating you lately, Rowan," which gave me a *bit* of a clue.

But don't get me wrong; it's not like I instantly got all excited and thought me and Erin would be best friends for ever again. It's more like there's been some big blister of *oddness* between us, and now – after what happened at the ice rink – the blister is burst and we both know what's going on, even if we haven't said the exact words out loud.

What I *know* is that outside the classroom, Erin will be hanging out with Ingrid and Yaz from now on.

As for *inside* the classroom, I'm pretty sure that we'll probably *still* sit together – till the summer holidays, I reckon – since teachers will want to know what's going on if we don't, and that's a conversation neither of us would love to have in public.

And next term? I shouldn't think so.

Then when it comes to the summer holidays themselves. . . Well, there'll be no more me and Erin hanging out, watching movies, or going on day trips to the beach with her dad Dave and mum Gillian. (*Wow*, I'm going to miss Dave and Gillian! I've just realized I've always had a bit of a Hero Crush on them *both*, for being Very Cool Parent Types.)

Anyway, it wasn't just Erin who turned on the apologetic niceness today. I'd got something *badly* wrong, and needed to fix it.

After assembly this morning, Kerise Bennett said, "Hey, has anyone heard? They caught the people doing all the graffiti in the temporary toilets! It's two Year Eight girls; Mrs Wells wandered into the loos to check them and caught Ellie Fisher and Vicky Harrison writing *'Zoe Clark looks like a melon in a wig!'*"

I don't really know those two Year Eight girls much, but they obviously had opinions on a whole heap of people (including me) at school.

I guess what's most important is that if Ellie and Vicky from Year Eight were the grafitti scrawlers, it meant Ingrid and Yaz most definitely DIDN'T scribble my own personal graffiti nasty.

Why'd I thought they *had*?

'Cause I was jealous of them hanging out with Erin, and wanted to believe the worst about them, I suppose. . .

Once I sussed that out, I immediately decided that *ALWAYS say you're sorry when you've made a mistake* would be a great Raspberry Rule, but as I don't have any room inside my frame to scribble it on, I won't bother.

Still, the important thing is, I've now said sorry to Ingrid and Yaz.

Nearly.

Because I am a complete chicken, I asked Erin to do it *for* me. (I know, I'm useless.)

Monday 12.46 p.m.

Oops.

Just did something that felt like the RIGHT thing to do before I did it, and then felt deeply WRONG as soon as I finished.

I'm in the library, and I have just this second sent an email that said. . .

Dear Sacha Fairy,

Thank you for getting back to me when I wrote to you about my best friend problem, even if it was just to say that you couldn't help (unless it was a tutu query).

I know I shouldn't have written you a personal email, because at school we're always being taught about how to be safe online, and sending you a message with my personal email address

on it was a definite big no-no, and I shouldn't
have done it.
Please don't be offended – it's not that I think
you're a a psychotic, cyberspace-prowling
weirdo or anything.
Love,
Rowan Love
P.S. Don't mean to be impatient or ungrateful,
but you mentioned at the bottom of your last
email that a sprinkling of fairy dust would waft
my way, and it doesn't seem to have arrived yet.

Why did I think that was a good idea? (Maybe my brain is misfiring after an emotional morning.)

Whatever, writing to the Find Your Inner Fairy website illegally (for the second time), I have betrayed Miss Whyte's trust *again*.

And I have probably insulted an innocent customer services fairy too.

If Linn found out, she would say that was "*BEYOND IDIOTIC, EVEN FOR YOU*, ROWAN!!"

Monday 12.48 p.m.
Whoooo!

Just as I was twisting myself in knots with guilt there, I

looked up and saw Libby-Mae Ferguson standing RIGHT behind me, waiting for a computer to come free!!

As I stood up, I *swear* she looked at me and sort of . . . *smiled*! (Yay! Now I'm not normal, I've suddenly become *visible* to her!!)

But that's not the best bit. No, no, *no*!

The best bit was the fact that she SPOKE TO ME!!! !!!

I'll never forget those seven magic words. . .

"Hey, what've you done to your arm?" she asked, pointing to my screamingly obvious pink plaster cast.

Whatever started it, it was a *brilliant* conversation, with us chatting about the circumstances behind my broken wrist, her happiness at me handing over her much-treasured, lost-but-found brooch, and us finishing with a plan to go to Saturday's Fairy Fun Day together.

Ha, ha, ha!!!

Nope, it went more like this: I squeaked, "Broke my wrist!", felt my cheeks go as pink as my plaster cast, and then ran off with my beaded school bag clattering against every metal-edged chair in the library.

Linn's right; I am *such* a dingbat.

Rowan Dingbat Love, *that's* me.

Monday 4.45 p.m.

OK, it was all change for our recycling group today.

Instead of heading to the Reuse and Recycling Centre and meeting them there, our Alexandra Hill buddies were coming here to *our* school, so we could take over half the art department and print up Marlon and Yusuf's Bag Bags.

The only thing was, they were super-late, which was OK and kind of fun, 'cause me and William and Marlon and Verity got to goof around a bit.

William said, "Hey, brilliant, Rowan; you've gone back to looking nuts!" when he saw me.

"*You* can talk about looking nuts!" I said back to him, since he'd just made himself a handlebar moustache out of scrap black paper from the art desk and stuck it on with double-sided tape.

Miss Boyle was out of the room phoning the other school to check that our buddies and the teaching assistant who was bringing them hadn't fallen into a previously unknown ravine on the way here.

"Apparently, there's been an incident, and they left late," Miss Boyle said with a frown when she came back in, then burst out laughing when she saw the four of us turn round and look at her with matching handlebar moustaches. (Verity's was on upside down – she'd run

239

around the art desks squealing, "*Nooooo!!* Don't you dare! And if you dare I'm *sooooo* going to tell, so you'd better not put that moustache *anywhere* near me!!" etc., etc., before the rest of us caught her, pinned her down giggling and stuck it on.)

Anyway, that was all Miss Boyle knew about the Alexandra Hill crew, but then as soon as Georgie, Bianca, Yusuf and Omar *finally* turned up, she and their teaching assistant had this hushed little conversation, the type you *know* means it's a teacher-only, X-rated-for-students type thing.

Not that it stopped me from asking Georgie what was going on the *second* Miss Boyle sent me and Georgie off to get more screen-printing inks.

Specially since I'd seen Bianca squeeze Georgie's arm and give her a wink just now.

"So, what was this 'incident' thingy that made you all late?" I said straight out.

"I got called to see the head teacher," said Georgie, chewing on her lip and staring at the handlebar moustache that I now had stuck to my hair like a floppy paper bow.

Wait a second.

Georgie had been called to see her head teacher?! Super-shy Georgie?

Usually people get hauled in to see the head for a *bad* reason. But if we were talking Georgie, it must have been for a *good* reason, right? Like getting a ton of extra merits for being involved in the Big Bring-&-Swap Party or something, maybe?

"So how come your head wanted to see you?"

Georgie bit her lip some more. Weirdly, she looked like a mixture of EMBARRASSED and PLEASED at my question.

(But I guess it was no more weird than me feeling BRILLIANT and AWFUL when I got up this morning.)

"Uh, remember those two lads who were making a fool of my mum on Saturday?" Georgie answered, as she stood around awkwardly while I opened the art resource room.

"Yeah, sure! Cameron and somebody, wasn't it?!"

"And Kurt. Well . . . when *they* were in the dinner hall this lunch time, I sneaked into the cloakroom and sewed the sleeves of their jackets closed. . ."

!!!!!!!!!!!!!!!!!!!!!!!!!!!!!!!

No *wonder* Bianca was squeezing her arm just now.

Oh, I'm so PROUD!

Can you believe it?!

Little old *me* taught my buddy Georgie a form of SELF-DEFENCE!!!

Wow, what would she be capable of if I taught her how to *knit*?

Monday 6.10 p..m.

Grandma came into my room a few minutes ago, just before she headed home to her flat.

"Thought I'd see what you've done with the flowers!" she said cheerfully. I'd made another paper bouquet – this time out of shiny, bright Sunday supplement magazines – while *she* was making cottage pie tonight, and *I* was supposed to be listening to her explain how to do it. (Mince, mash, and, er, blah, blah, blah.)

I'd stuck my flowers in an empty fabric conditioner bottle (lavender) and had them sitting on my bedside table, next to my twin photo frame made out of shells, with the picture of Mum on one side and Johnny Depp on the other.

"Looking good," Grandma murmured, nodding, while she gazed around at *all* my über-colourful stuff and tons of kitsch bits and bobs. Grandma's flat is all beige and minimal. I know my room makes her feel a bit dizzy. "And *this* in particular. . ."

Here's the funny thing; Grandma pretended to look at the Raspberry Rules as if she'd never seen them before. (Yeah, like she hasn't noticed them when she's been hoovering glitter out of my carpet or whatever.)

"Did you always feel this way, Rowan?" she asked.

At first, I thought Grandma was pointing at Rule No. 13 (*"I will NOT put rubbish out while only wearing out-of-date pants. . ."*), which made me a bit confused, till I realized her finger had slipped and she was actually pointing at No. 18, i.e., the squashed-in one at the bottom about getting myself a new best friend. I only wrote that this morning. She must have spotted it when she was dusting or something today.

"I mean, have you always felt that Erin was embarrassed and annoyed by you, dear?"

"Um, sometimes," I shrugged, thinking that *everyone* often was, not just Erin.

"Is that why you tried to dress so differently last week?" Grandma asked, coming over to sit beside me on my bed.

OK, *I* got it. Coming up here to check out the flowers was a ruse; she just wanted to have a private grandmother-granddaughter chat; to see how I was feeling about Erin and being best-friend-less.

"Uh, yeah. . . I thought she might like me better that way," I told her.

"Rowan, darling, you shouldn't change the way you

are just for someone else," said Grandma, suddenly sounding a lot like Miss Boyle as she reached out and held my hands. "If Erin didn't like you for who you were, then she wasn't a very good best friend to start with, was she?"

"But Erin was my only really good friend!" I told her back.

"Rowan, with friends like that, who needs enemies?" she answered, looking me meaningfully in the eye.

I didn't know what she meant exactly, because I was . . .

a) remembering that other phrase Grandma used to always say about me and Erin – something about opposites attracting, and . . .
b) slightly distracted by the sight of Fluffy washing her bum. Cats are so incredibly *bendy*, aren't they?

Then I realized that Grandma was *still* looking at me meaningfully over the top of her gold-rimmed glasses. It sort of unnerved me, as if she'd be able to read my mind any second and suss out that I hadn't been paying attention.

So I quickly pulled my magazine flower bouquet out of the fabric conditioner bottle vase and said, "Here; for *you*, Grandma!"

"Oh, Rowan! Thank you!" she said with a small, uncertain smile.

I knew she appreciated the gesture. But *now* she'd have to stress about where to put them in her minimal, beige flat.

(The bin?)

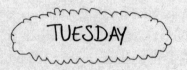

TUESDAY

Tuesday 7:49 a.m.

Made a wish on my inner fairy for a new best friend.

Shouldn't have kissed it for luck – got glitter on my lips and it made my peanut butter on toast a bit too crunchy.

Tuesday 8.55 a.m.

Whoo! I'm so pleased – I just got hold of Miss Boyle and it turns out she HASN'T taken all the leftover stuff from the Big Bring-&-Swap Party to the dump yet.

That is SO excellent, because I was lying in bed last night, worrying that I might have the squirrel pants dream again, when I remembered that I'd woken up yesterday morning staring *straight* at Ally's sky-and-clouds duvet cover.

It was bugging me; I just couldn't figure what exactly my secret sleepwalk meant. . .

Then I got it; it was something to do with the rainbow made of rubbish!

I could make that for *real*, with squirrel knick-knacks for the brown arc, and all the other colours made up from the broken, useless, plastic toy bits and bobs that no one wanted.

!!!

Miss Boyle says it's an *amazing* idea and the Rubbish Rainbow can go on the front of our stall on Saturday as our centrepiece, along with a pile of William and Omar's recycling centre leaflets, Marlon and Yusuf's Bag Bags, plus a board showing photos of the Big Bring-&-Swap Party and details of how people can run one themselves.

That is *so* cool.

What's *not* so cool is that it makes it harder for me to AVOID going to the exhibition in the Town Hall Square now, but I really, *really* MUST go to the Fairy Fun Day in Trafalgar Square.

Aarghhhh. . .!

CRAFT INSTRUCTIONS

Rubbish rainbow

You'll need:

- Little bits of tiny plastic tat, like old pocket-money toys or lids off bottles
- Strong glue
- A sheet of thick cardboard

Instructions:

1) Gather lots and lots of tiny plastic tat, and separate them into piles of the same colours.
2) Cut out a rainbow shape from a large sheet of cardboard and draw separate sections for each colour you're using.
3) Stick the tiny plastic tat on with strong glue in arcs of colour.
4) Make a wish on your own personal planet-saving rainbow!

Tuesday 12.37 p.m.

WEIRD ALERT!! WEIRD ALERT!! WEIRD ALERT!!

I'm in the library and I just picked up a reply from Sacha Fairy! Here's the message. . .

Dear Customer,

Thank you for your email. Your online security and safety are very important to us.

May we remind you that customers to this site should be over 18, or contacting us ONLY with the permission of parents/guardian.

All the best,

Sacha Fairy (Customer Services)

"May a sprinkle of fairy dust waft your way with this email!"

P.S. Check out Jacqui Fairy's all-new blog!!

To be honest, when I first read that I felt a bit flat. That's 'cause it made me feel guilty all over again for going against school rules AND 'cause it suddenly dawned on me (doh!) that the "*sending a sprinkle of fairy dust*" thing was just a tagline that must go at the bottom of *all* Sacha Fairy's customer emails. Yep, it *hadn't* been a personal message meant just for me. Sigh.

But then I clicked back on to the home page and read Jacqui Fairy's blog entry, and felt PROPERLY goose-pimply!

After saying a sparkly hello and reminding everyone about the Fairy Fun Day this Saturday, she'd written. . .

And can I finish with this thought:
If you ever feel lonely, try to be your OWN best
friend.
Believe in yourself, because you are so fantastic
and unique!
Think fluffy thoughts, and let colour light your way. . .
Jacqui Fairy xxx

HOW spooky is *that*?

With that last bit about being your own best friend
. . . it's like it's meant just for *me*!

And I mean, I'm *already* trying to be more colourful,
by going pink this week! (Apart from the lipgloss
eyeshadow – I've given that up since my fringe kept
getting stuck in it yesterday.)

Wow, I am *so* goose-pimply!

I really hope Miss Whyte the librarian doesn't notice
or she'll either know telepathically that I have broken
school rules, or else she'll assume I've got a strange
tropical bump disease and send me to the school nurse.

Tuesday 12.39 p.m.

Arghh!! I have bumps on my *goosebumps*! I'm one huge
quivering girl bump!!!

I was just thinking a mad thought: did Sacha the

Customer Services Fairy tell Jacqui the Big Boss Fairy about my first email? Is that friendship advice in the blog there to help *me*?!

Arghh again!! Maybe I *am* going mad, but I am *definitely* going to the Fun Day now, so I can meet Jacqui Fairy and Sacha Fairy in person. (I'm going to start designing some wings tonight.)

I'm shaking so much, I need to sit down.

Oh, I already *am* sitting down.

Wednesday 8.19 a.m.

Sometimes I get my head in knots, and it takes someone *much* more mature than me to untangle them.

This morning, it was my eleven-year-old sister.

Ally caught me about half an hour ago with my head in the bathroom sink, all because my mind had been in such a muddle that I'd started combing through my hair with my toothbrush (and toothpaste).

She helped wash the toothpaste out, and then made me sit on the edge of the bath and tell her what was wrong. There were actually *four* wrong things, and they were (in order of stressfulness)...

1) **The squirrel knickers dream**. I'd had it again. *This* time, I was running down the street I didn't know, only there were crowds on either side of the road laughing at me, all wearing masks with Erin's face on

them (!). I was shouting at them/her to leave me alone when I suddenly woke up with Rolf jumping on the bed to sniff my plaster cast and Fluffy hissing and yowling at him.

2) **Fluffy's dislike of all the other pets**. She just won't leave my room. Or specifically, the safety of my pants drawer.

3) **Clashing events**. I want to go to the Fairy Fun Day on Saturday but can't 'cause it's happening on the same day as the recycling exhibition in the Town Hall Square.

4) **No best friend**. How will I get over losing Erin?

Once I burbled all that (in a much longer, rambling way, believe me), Ally blinked at me for a second, as if she was trying to figure out how someone with a head full of fuzz ever managed to concentrate on homework and exams. (I wonder too.)

"Right, well, Fluffy's easy," she said, folding herself up so she was sitting cross-legged on the toilet seat lid. "If she feels safe in your pants drawer, just *move* the pants drawer downstairs to the living room, where the other pets are. She'll get used to them that way, in a place where she's secure."

(Well, who'd have guessed my humble pants had

such an important mission to fulfil?)

Next, Ally moved on to my clashing events on Saturday.

"What time is the recycling exhibition?" Ally checked with me.

"Um, ten till twelve," I told her.

"So when's the Fun Day on?"

"All day, I think," I told her.

"Then go to it *after* the recycling exhibition, Ro!" Ally laughed at me, as if I was a cute but dense amoeba.

She really is a genius. (I must remember to give her back the shoelace from her favourite pair of Converse trainers. . .)

With the squirrel knickers dream, Ally said she'd need to think about it and get back to me. (Even eleven-year-old geniuses have their limits.)

"But what about Erin?" I asked her, wondering what Ally's genius take on best friends was. "How can anyone take her place?"

"Easily!" laughed Ally; then she threw Tor's wet whale sponge at me and ran away.

(OK, so she *is* sometimes more of a kid than me.)

Wednesday 12.48 p.m.
I got goosebumps in the library again!

But for a TOTALLY different reason this time.

I couldn't get on a computer to see if there were any new, meaningful blog posts on the Find Your Inner Fairy website, because annoyingly, other students were using them all for legitimate coursework. Pah! (*Wish* I could win that laptop from last week's *Hornsey Journal*, though it'll probably be the dandruff shampoo, knowing my luck.)

Anyway, I was impatiently hovering in the Ancient Civilizations section, pretending to be interested in a book about Pompeii, when I saw Libby-Mae Ferguson wander *out* of the Older Teenage section and *over* to Miss Whyte to get some book scanned out to her.

Of course, I was right there in a second, getting the Pompeii book scanned out too.

I was SO close, I could smell Libby-Mae's rosy perfume, and *she* could probably smell the dog food curry I'd dipped my shirt sleeve into by accident in the dinner hall just now.

She was *definitely* close enough to spot the funny little lump in my blazer lapel, *and* the silver fastening there too. Though she might need to have X-ray eyes to see the fairy brooch secretly hiding on the *reverse* of my lapel.

"Pompeii? Scary stuff, eh?" she said, tapping my book.

EEEK! She talked to me again!!!

"Mmmm. . ." I nodded, not having a clue what was supposed to be scary about Pompeii.

"See you, then!!"

"Mmmm!"

OK, so the conversation wasn't exactly scintillating (good use of vocabulary; tick!), specially from *my* side. But it was the *next* bit that got me goosebumping. . .

"Loving that colour, by the way!"

She was pointing at the plaster cast. Then she was gone.

And *that's* when the goosebumps started.

I mean, I *know* that my big sister Linn is right and I am absolutely an idiot and mad and possibly crazier than William Smith (who I saw this morning walking along the science block hallway on his hands) but wasn't that comment a little *spooky*?

Think about it. . .

"Loving that colour!" she'd said.

"*Think fluffy thoughts, and always let colour light your way. . .*" it said on the Find Your Inner Fairy blog.

Coincidence? Or not?!

I mean, Libby-Mae Ferguson *did* accidentally drop that Find Your Inner Fairy leaflet on the library floor a couple of weeks or so ago? Or had she *meant* for me to find it? And what about the fairy brooch? Was that meant for me to have too, like some coded message?

As Alice in Wonderland said (I think), it's all getting curiouser and curiouser. . .

Wednesday 5 p.m.

Did you know that that Pompeii's famous 'cause a volcano called Vesuvius in Roman times killed thousands and thousands of people? And that the lava and stuff from the volcano hit the town so hard, lots of people were mummified in ash where they were?!

Georgie had come around to mine to help make the Rubbish Rainbow, but started by reading that out to me from my library book while I was sorting hundreds of tiny plastic toy bits and bobs into colours.

(She's made me promise to take out more history books for her from my school library, as she's read all the ones in Alexandra Hill library, and she's too scared to go to Wood Green public library ever since the family got asked to leave because McKenzie, Sapphire and Romany got orangey Wotsits fingerprints on most of the books in the under-five section.)

The two of us were out in the garden, with a big cardboard arch (cut out of packaging Dad had in his shop) laid out flat on the lawn.

Naturally, Linn shouted, "THERE IS NO *BROWN* IN

THE RAINBOW!!!" when she saw me gluing the squirrel knick-knacks on to the arch.

I asked her back if she'd ever heard of the term "artistic licence", and she got all huffy and went away.

Georgie sniggered.

Y'know, I know it was sort of a *dumb* thing to do, but I think there's something a little bit *different* about Georgie since she sewed up the sleeves of those doughball lads in her class.

(By the way, while *Georgie* got into trouble – obviously – Cameron and Karl got into a whole lot *more* when Georgie explained to the head teacher exactly WHY she'd been busy with a darning needle.)

Anyway, same as me and Erin's friendship, it's like some kind of a blister's burst for Georgie, but this particular blister* had all her shyness inside it, I think.

And maybe that made me open up to her more.

Which – I guess – is a posh way of saying that I went and I told her that I am possibly *insane* and suspect that an older girl at my school MIGHT be acting like my guardian angel, and (erm) could be trying somehow to help me out with my problems through a fairy website.

(Arrgh, that sounds super-crazy when I read it back. . .)

"So, uh, what do you think?" I asked her, once I'd spilled it all out.

Sitting cross-legged in her Arsenal football shirt, Georgie blinked and frowned hard, though I took it as a good sign that she didn't snort at me (think Erin would've).

But whatever she was thinking never got said, 'cause of Ally suddenly appearing in the garden and ordering me to SET THE SQUIRREL KNICKERS ON FIRE.

||||||||||||||||||||||||||||||||||||||||||||||||||||||||||

"In my considered opinion," my little sister announced, in her best Dr Ally Love, Top Psychology Expert voice (which sounded a little bit like a snooty owl), "the squirrel knickers dream means you need to *move* on from your ex-friendship, and only *then* will your nightmares stop."

"How do I do that, then?" I asked her.

"Aha!" said Dr Love, now sounding like a mad scientist. "We've got to have a ceremonial Burning of the Pants!!"

It was only then that I realized Dr Love had the squirrel knickers and a box of kitchen matches hidden behind her back.

It was excellent – I lit the match (under Grandma's slightly frowning, watchful eye), and in two seconds flat, we had our own small pyre on the rusty barbeque that Dad hasn't dropped off at the dump yet.

The only ones who *didn't* get into the knicker BBQ were Mr and Mrs Misery-Guts from next door, who came out into their garden to cough loudly (Grandma said to ignore them), and Rolf and Winslet, who'd assumed there'd be burgers.

---

* All this talking about blisters is making me feel a bit sick. Will have to think of a better analogy**.

** Good vocabulary; tick!

Wednesday 9.30 p.m.

Still sniggering about the ceremonial Burning of the Pants.

Still thinking exceptionally mad thoughts about Libby-Mae Ferguson being involved with the Find Your Inner Fairy website. Jacqui Fairy only looks like she's in her twenties or something. Maybe she's Libby-Mae's big *sister*! And Sacha Fairy could be *another* big sister, or a cool auntie maybe!!! A whole family of fairies!!! Guess I'll soon find out, when I go to the Fairy Fun Day on Saturday. . .

Speaking of Saturday, I've been thinking about knitting a pair of fairy wings for my Fairy Fun Day costume and started with a prototype that was cat-sized. I stuck them on Fluffy earlier; but she started hissing, probably because she was sitting in a drawer full of pants – with home-made wings on – in the living room, in full view of all the other pets. The shame!!!

Managed to take a photo before she clawed them off, though. Very cute.

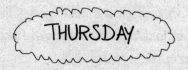
THURSDAY

Thursday 8.18 a.m.

Like my pants, I'm on fire!!!

Now that I know I can safely go to the recycling exhibition AND the Fairy Fun Day, I woke up this morning and decided to go craft crazy!! For our stall on Saturday, I'm going bring along my . . .

- sweetie hairgrips,
- newspaper flowers,
- beady bag,
- skinny scarf (now stitched back together, with ribbon threaded through the repair),
- the pet leg warmers (modelled on one of Tor's fluffy toys),
- an empty frame (to show how you can display 3D art),
- the mini memory shrine,

- my fake flower crash helmet, and . . .
- this covered journal with my patchwork inner fairy (will have to cut out and stick a new face on it, to hide the beard and glasses).

I will type out instructions on how to do all the crafts and photocopy them to hand out!

Don't quite know what happened to me in the night*, but something sure made me wake up with my head whirling with positive thoughts.

What I *do* know is that I didn't have the squirrel-knicker dream – yay! Mind you, I *did* have a dream that my new middle name was "Graham". Not sure what that was about, unless I'm now being haunted by the ghost of Graham the Snail Take One. . .

* Maybe some fairy dust fluttered through my bedroom window after all?!

Thursday 10.32 a.m.
In French today, Erin asked me how I was doing, and I said, "Great!!!" in this over-the-top way that made her crinkle the freckles on her nose uncomfortably, as if she thought I was hiding my True Deep Sorrow at the end of our friendship.

The trouble is, I really *do* feel GREAT!! I can't wait till lunch time – that's 'cause I am going to . . .

a) type up my recycling craft sheets on a library computer, and . . .
b) find Libby-Mae Ferguson and somehow very subtly let her know that I MIGHT know who she's related to!

Ooh, just heard a humming outside of this cubicle that I recognize!!

Have an idea – back in a minute.

Thursday 10.35 a.m.
The humming belonged to Linn.

She rolled her eyes when I bounced out of the cubicle – well, actually, *after* I'd pushed open the other cubicle doors so I knew we were alone.

"WHAT ARE YOU UP TO? CHECKING FOR SECRET AGENTS?!" she asked.

"No way!" I said, trying to laugh casually. (It sounded like I'd sucked a helium balloon.) "But listen, I was just wondering. . ."

"NO – I CAN'T LEND YOU ANY MONEY. OR CLOTHES. OR ANYTHING ELSE, RO," said Linn firmly, smoothing back her already perfectly smoothed hair in the mirror above the sink.

"I don't want to borrow anything," I said quickly, before anyone else came in and spoiled my moment of opportunity. "I just. . ."

My scatty brain failed me. I wanted to ask her a series of *very* subtle questions about Libby-Mae Ferguson, but I couldn't think of one subtle thing to ask. The only thing my scatty brain could come up with was. . .

"Linn, do you happen to know if Libby-Mae's got a sister who's a fairy?"

"RO!! HAVE YOU BEEN INHALING *GLITTER* OR SOMETHING?!" Linn frowned at me. "LOOK, *ALL* I KNOW ABOUT LIBBY-MAE FERGUSON IS THAT SHE LIVES IN ONE OF THOSE HOUSES IN THE CUL-DE-SAC BY THE FIRE STATION. OK? CAN I GO NOW, AND ESCAPE YOUR STRANGENESS IN CASE IT'S INFECTIOUS?!"

Of course she could.

It was all I needed.

Thursday 4.10 p.m.

I've been sitting on the wall outside the fire station for thirty-five minutes now, trying to act casual.

The firemen have been watching me as they wash their fire engines, and laughing. Maybe they think I am someone who has a crush on firemen. I think those tend to be women over forty, but maybe they're assuming I'm starting a few decades early.

So far there's no sign of Libby-Mae, and no sign of anyone who looks like Jacqui Fairy coming in or out of any of the houses on the cul-de-sac. (By the way, d'you think Jacqui off of the Find Your Inner Fairy website dresses like a fairy *all* the time? Would she still wear her wings and make-up and mini tutu getting out of a Ford Mondeo with Tesco shopping bags?!)

Whatever, I'm just going to carry on either writing in this journal or pretending I'm getting a stone out of my shoe till I get some kind of evidence.

Thursday 5.30 p.m.

I'd just been getting lost in this mad doodle for about five minutes when someone sat down beside me on the wall.

I nearly jumped out of my flip-flops.

"Hi, Rowan! What are you doing?" said Marlon's laid-back voice.

"Um, just drawing," I said in a tense, guilty squeak. "What are *you* doing here?"

"I live in a flat over there –" he pointed to a 1930s block on the opposite side of the road from the cul-de-sac and the fire station "– and I've been watching you for about an hour, scribbling stuff and fiddling with your feet."

"What – so you've been *spying* on me?" I said all defensively.

Which was mad, in the circumstances, since I was on a spying mission myself.

Marlon just shrugged, unperturbed.

"So what are you doing round here?" he asked finally, after a minute's silence that had made me start to sweat.

What was I supposed to answer to that? "I am stalking Libby-Mae Ferguson," or "I think she might have fairies in her family"???

So I said something that was the truth, if not the whole truth.

"My big sister told me Libby-Mae Ferguson lives round here. I've got something of hers to give back. Have you seen her?"

"Nope," said Marlon.

"Do you know which house is hers?"

"Yep," he replied, in an infuriatingly minimal way.

"Well, which one is it?" I demanded, with a slightly squeaky desperation in my voice.

"The one with the blue door. Where her mum's coming out."

With my heart badum-badumming madly in my chest, I spun around — to see a skinny dark-haired woman coming out with a black bin liner in her hand and a screaming toddler dressed in blue in the other.

"Has she got any *other*, erm, brothers or sisters, do you know?" I asked, as casually as I could.

"Uh . . . yeah. Older, though," said Marlon, unaware of how much my heart was suddenly pounding.

"How old?" I asked, imagining Jacqui or Sacha Fairy fluttering from their fairy flat to their old family home for a visit.

"He's about twenty or whatever. Screeches around here on his motorbike, bugging half the neighbours."

Thunk went my hopes of Libby-Mae having a fairy for a sister, along with the *thunk* of the bin lid.

But still . . . she *was* connected to the Find Your Inner Fairy website *somehow*. I just needed to find out how exactly.

"What do you need to give her back?" Marlon asked, fixing me with one of his penetrating stares.

He really does do staring very well. I was pretty unnerved.

"Hmmm? Oh. . ." I mumbled, flipping my lapel over to show him what was pinned there.

"This brooch. I saw her drop it."

Ace excuse! Ten out of ten points to *me*!!

"Wouldn't it be easier just to see her at school?" asked Marlon, stretching his arms lazily behind his head.

Marlon might not have known he was doing it, but he was making things *very* difficult for me.

At that moment I felt my panic goblin thunder up on a stepladder from my chest to my head, stopping me from coming up with any *reasonable* excuse that made the *tiniest* bit of sense with all that racket. So I said something AWFUL instead.

"Is it true you got expelled from your last school for supergluing your head teacher's door shut?"

"Uh, yeah," nodded Marlon, after thinking about it for a second.

"But why?" I pushed him, embarrassed at asking the question but feeling like I couldn't stop now.

"Well, he didn't ever believe my mum when she said

my kid sister was getting bullied. It was great watching him have to escape out the window. Till I got expelled and my mum went *mental* at me."

Wow. I blinked at him open-mouthed. It was like Georgie sewing Cameron and Karl's sleeves shut, times fifty.

And it was one of those clashes of two opposites, wasn't it? Like Georgie, he'd done a BAD thing for a GOOD reason. He'd been BRAVE but STUPID at the same time.

Just like *I* was being BRAVE but STUPID hanging about round Libby-Mae's house, thinking no one would spot me (though I may be hard to miss).

"Hey," said Marlon, disturbing my mulling. "Isn't that what's-er-face right there?"

Oh my gosh, it was!!! Libby-Mae Ferguson glided by us, like an auburn-haired swan*.

"Aren't you gonna—" Marlon began.

"Nah, I . . . uh. . ." I mumbled, feeling the bravery slipping away, and stupidity creeping in.

("Hi, Libby-Mae, is this your brooch?" "Why yes! But how did you know where I lived?" "Because I'm stalking you!! Now can you tell me if you and your inner fairy are watching over me?")

"Hey, she's going—" said Marlon, about to stick two

fingers in either side of his mouth and give a ginormous whistle.

NOOOOOOO!!!

"It's OK!" I yelped, yanking his hands down with both of mine. "I've just remembered something really important!!"

I must have yelped too loud. Out of the corner of my eye, I saw Libby-Mae spin her crinkly waves of luscious long hair round to glance at us.

Yeah, to glance at me and Marlon *holding hands* . . . 'cause *that's* what it must have looked like from where she was gliding.

"Remembered *what* something important?" Marlon laughed at me, all laid-back as usual.

That I'm an idiot, I thought.

"That I'm an idiot," my mouth said out loud, before my brain had a chance to think of something smarter.

I heard Marlon still laughing as I hurried flip-flap-flopping off past the fire station and towards home. . .

And now here I am, quietly shrivelling into a ball of embarrassment, while squeezing Fluffy too tight.

* Does that analogy work? Or does it just sound like a big bird in a wig?

FRIDAY

Friday 7.30 a.m.

Fluffy has forgiven me for excess hugging last night, and is still in one piece. I'm about to carry her downstairs to the living room in the pants drawer, as Ally's theory seems to be working, and Fluffy is allowing the other pets to come up and sniff her in her Royal Pants Drawer without hissing at them.

I'm feeling different about Marlon this morning too. In the panic of yesterday, I thought he was making things tricky for me and laughing at me, but really — without him knowing — he saved me from being branded as a mad, crazed stalker. (A hero *again*!!)

Not that I'm going to tell him, because I may never be able to look him in the eye after shouting "I'm an idiot!" in front of him very loudly.

Eeek!

Friday 8.35 a.m.

WOW, WOW, WOW!!

 I WON THE LAPTOP COMPUTER!!!

The postman delivered it just now!

Unfortunately, I won't be able to look up the Find Your Inner Fairy website, as I didn't read the description properly, and didn't realize it was a little kids' PRETEND laptop, complete with Tweenie-style *"HELLO!! DO YOU WANT TO PLAY?!"* screechy vocals on it.

Winslet was sniffing at it just now. It's a bit big for her, but has a glittery logo on the top, so she *may* have a go at stealing it away and giving it a chew under someone's bed.

Can't say I care – it would've been better if I'd won the dandruff shampoo.

Or even the Bratz Hawaiian Nail Salon . . . there might have been real nail polish in there that I could have used.

Friday 8.59 a.m.

Turned a corner towards class right now and nearly bumped straight into William Smith, who was juggling the contents of his packed lunch (an apple, a can of Pepsi and a slightly squashed roll in cellophane).

Marlon was right behind him.

"Hey, Rowan!" said William, never taking his eyes off his rotating lunch.

"Uh, hi..." I muttered back to them both, waiting for what was coming next, which would be something along the lines of "So what's it like being an idiot? Ha, ha, ha!", since Marlon was *bound* to have told him all about yesterday.

But nothing more came, and William carried on carefully juggling off to his class, with Marlon ambling after him.

Then Marlon gave me a grin and a wink.

So does that mean that my general idiotness will stay between us?

I guess so ... I guess Marlon is the sort of quiet guy who's a good keeper of secrets. After all, he managed to keep *his* – about the story behind the superglue saga – all to himself (till yesterday).

Just to let Marlon know that I wouldn't be blabbing either, I quickly winked back.

Only the fluster I was in meant I got in a momentary panic about which eye to blink, so I did *both*, first one, then the other.

Which probably made me look like an idiot. (No change there, then.)

Friday 12.50 p.m.

Big shock outside the Female Visitors' Toilets just now.

Taped to the door was a sign that said, "*Would all students refrain from using these toilets now that the main ones are back in use downstairs.*"

Boo!!!

What would I do without my little office; i.e., the far-left cubicle?

How dull would school toilet breaks be now with zero fake flower displays, soft coloured loo roll and lily of the valley hand wash?!

Though I wasn't going to be the *only* one in mourning.

"S'cuse!"

I smelled Libby-Mae Ferguson's rosy perfume as she swooped up the corridor towards me and the loos, like the sweet-smelling possibly fairy princess that she was.

"We're not allowed to g-go in there," I told her, stumbling over the most coherent sentence I'd ever come up with in her presence.

This close up, she was so tall and perfect and gorgeous, just everything a small, not-very-perfect or gorgeous girl could ever dream of being.

(*Please* let her only have seen me and Marlon "holding hands". *Please* don't let her have heard me yelling about being an idiot.)

"Hmmm?" said Libby-Mae, blinking her huge, glittery-green eyelids at me.

"It's back to being for female visitors only," I told her, tapping on the sign so that my pink plaster cast thunked on the door.

Idiotness and nerves aside, I knew that *now* was the moment. The moment for *everything*. . .

But where would I start? Probably with something small.

"Is, um, this yours?" I suddenly asked, flipping back my lapel, proud of the fact that my voice was only wobbling a little bit.

Libby-Mae leant forward and squinted at the brooch I was pulling free.

"Oh, *that*?" she muttered, and started laughing. "It's one of those stupid charity things; you donate a pound and you get a badge or whatever. My nana's *always* a mug for those, and then always gives *me* the dopey things!"

Libby-Mae took the brooch from me, looked at it, and wobbled the broken wing.

"Rubbish, isn't it?" she said, kicking the door of the

Female Visitors' Toilets open with her patent-leather orange ballet pumps *just* wide enough to chuck the brooch into the bin under the sink.

"Thanks anyway!" she giggled, in a shrieky voice that was spookily like the Tweenie-style voice on the toy laptop all of a sudden, and not the elegant, melodic lilt I'd got in my head.

?!

With a head fluffy with nerves and confusion, my mouth suddenly asked a question I didn't expect.

"Uh . . . do you know . . . um . . . *Sacha*?" I found myself asking point blank, ever hopeful that I'd got it right, even though I was quickly beginning to think that maybe I hadn't.

"Sacha? Do you mean Sacha McClusky in Year Twelve? Gawd, *no*! I heard she's a *total* b—"

Oh.

The next word she said wasn't a very fairyish word, for sure.

"Hey, *I* know you!" Libby-Mae suddenly squeaked, pointing a fake fingernail at me. "*You're* Linn Love's freaky little sister, aren't you?"

"Mmm," I mumbled, not exactly loving her description.

"Can I ask you something?" she said, her eyes

twinkling with sudden excitement.

Close up, the glittery green eyeshadow and black eyeliner made her look more witchy than gorgeously pre-Raphaelite, now I came to think about it.

"Uh-huh," I mumbled warily.

"Is it true you keep four rats as pets and your mum's in prison?"

I think this week, I'd been secretly hoping that Libby-Mae Ferguson might equal a new best friend. I'd imagined that she was deep and interesting and a little bit magical, when really she was pretty but thick, and very possibly a little bit *mean*.

I didn't need to ask her if she had anything to do with the Find Your Inner Fairy website; I knew what the answer would be. (A big, fat *no*.)

"It's *cats*, and *no*," I managed to say as I flapped away fast in my flip-flops.

"Huh?" I heard Libby-Mae squawk behind me.

Wow.

How can Linn stand to have a sister like me?

I really am an *enormous* idiot. . .

Friday 1.14 p.m.

I'm an idiot, I'm an idiot.

How could I get it so wrong about Libby-Mae? How

could I be such a totally rubbish judge of character?!

I rushed from the Female Visitors' Toilets to modern studies, only to find a milling crowd of people waiting for Mr Svenson to open up the classroom. (Yes, it's unbelievable, but for once, I was ahead of the bell.)

With a whirling, thumping head, I leant up against a wall around the corner from everyone, only vaguely aware of the conversation going on around the corner from me.

"...and I thought maybe we should go?" I heard Erin suggest. "I mean, I know Rowan's been working on all her project stuff really hard, and we'd only have to hang about for a few minutes and say hi. It could be kind of fun!"

"Fun?! Seeing what Miss Boyle's oddballs-and-geeks group have been making in their 'special' sessions?" said someone who was *definitely* Yaz, and *definitely* giggling.

"Well, it's not really *like* that, is it?" I heard Erin argue in a wimpy sort of way.

"*Course* it's like that!" laughed Ingrid. "It's all the losers together! They're *all* weird, and that's why they were singled out! I mean, *Rowan's* nuts, William's all look-at-me! needy, Marlon's mostly silent and did something psycho at his last school, and Verity Smelly eats her *hair,* for gawd's sake!"

Everyone on the recycling project deserved for me to whip my head around right that second and blast off at Ingrid and Yaz.

I mean, I'm not *nuts!* Well, maybe a *little* bit, but in a nice way.

And so maybe William *is* all look-at-me! look-at-me! crazy, but so what?

Marlon might be quiet, but the "psycho" thing he did? Well, *I* know the story behind that and *I* know he is a good guy.

Verity is sweet and kind and dependable, even if she *does* eat her hair and doesn't get every joke in the world.

And as for our buddies from Alexandra Hill, what did Yaz and Ingrid know about *them*?! Were they all supposed to be oddballs and geeks too, just because they were not good at speaking English (Omar); very tiny (Bianca); super-smart (Yusuf) or ultra-shy (Georgie)?

Yeah, I *should* have blasted all that at Ingrid and Yaz. But my back felt as superglued against the wall as Marlon's ex-head teacher's door. My panic goblin was high-kicking in my chest, and one insistent thought kept sloshing round my head.

It was to do with my form teacher, Mrs Wells.

I thought she'd spotted something in me, and recommended me to Miss Boyle because I was different and special.

So now I've found out that I *was* chosen because I *was* different and special, but not in a good way.

Not in a good way at *all*. . .

Friday 8.07 p.m.

I'm an idiot, I'm an idiot, I'm an IDIOT.

The timings might work for me to do the recycling exhibition AND the Fairy Fun Day tomorrow, but I hadn't really figured on one VERY IMPORTANT thing.

"Honey, there's no *way* you can go into the West End of London on your own!" said Dad, when I showed him the wings I'd made just now.

Libby-Mae Ferguson might have as much to do with the fairies as Fluffy has with the Rottweiler Appreciation Society, but I still want to go to the Fun Day so badly. After all, the Find Your Inner Fairy website has been the only truly sparkly, special thing in my life over the last few weird weeks.

"Um . . . well, *could* you close your shop for a half-day and take me?" I tried, hopefully.

"Ro, shopkeepers can't let customers down; they

always have to stick to their opening hours. Especially skint shopkeepers like me!"

"But maybe Grandma can take me into town?"

"She's seeing friends on Saturday, remember?" said Dad. (I hadn't remembered.)

"What about Ally?"

"Ro, she's *eleven*!" Dad frowned, smiling at my desperate suggestion.

I thought about Linn for a second, and then realized that asking Linn to take me to a fairy rally would be like asking a crocodile to take a bunny to a butterfly farm. It just wouldn't be an option from the start.

So no Fairy Fun Day for me.

I'll just fold these wings up and stuff them under the bed and forget about them.

By the way, did I say that I'm an idiot???

CRAFT INSTRUCTIONS

Fairy wings

You'll need:

- 4 metal coat hangers, or about 2 metres of bendy but strong garden wire
- Nylon tights, 2 pairs

- Sequins, glitter and ribbons
- Elastic

Instructions:

1) Unbend the wire hangers (or garden wire), and rebend them into four teardrop shapes, twisting the wire at the teardrop ends all together, so that you've formed a butterfly-wing effect.

2) Tie two loops of elastic around this central wiry twist, big enough so that you can slide your arms through.

3) Cut four legs of tights (i.e., get rid of feet and bottom parts), and stretch each "leg" section over each teardrop wire shape, to make transparent wings, tying firmly in a knot at the "tip" of each wing, and stitching together in the middle, at the wiry twist.

4) Use sequins, glitter and ribbons to decorate, especially at the knotted and stitched areas, to make more fairy-licious!

SATURDAY

Saturday 7.42 a.m.

Had a bad dream about being trapped in a cardboard box, and woke up at ten past seven this morning . . . in a cardboard box.

!!!

It was one of the ones that Dad had taken home folded flat for my Rubbish Rainbow, and in my secret-sleepwalking mode, I'd managed to origami it into a standard box shape, stick it up right next to the TV, and climb inside it.

Not bad for an oddball geek with a broken wrist!

I jumped out as soon as I heard someone (it was Ally) coming downstairs.

"What's *that* for?" she yawned at me, and I quickly pretended I'd made a potential new hideaway for Fluffy, so that I could reclaim my pants drawer from the living room.

But I hadn't.

Actually, for about a split-second there, I thought I'd sleepwalked into the box because my subconscious was telling me I was *useless* by chucking me away inside something that was basically litter.

And THEN I sussed what it was *really* all about. Oh, yes . . . I'd actually just invented a piece of installation art!

A piece of installation art that will absolutely help Raise Awareness of Recycling in the Community at this morning's exhibition.

It'll be perfect! As long as none of the other oddball geeks object to looking as much of an idiot as me. But how could they? I practically have a neon halo that screams "I'M AN IDIOT!" above my head.

Saturday 12.10 p.m.

It was a total, FRANTIC rush to set up.

"It's all looking brilliant!!" Miss Boyle twittered, as she breathlessly positioned the Rubbish Rainbow at the front of our stall and set out the leaflets and information boards and Bag Bags.

Then there were all my crafts to display (the newspaper flowers, the mini memory shrine, etc., etc., and the info sheets I'd photocopied to go along with them).

Our stall was surrounded by stalls run by groups from other schools. (I narrowed my eyes at them to see if *they* looked like oddballs and geeks, but I couldn't tell, since I didn't think any of *us* looked like oddballs and geeks.)

Don't like to sound big-headed, but from what I could make out, none of theirs was *nearly* as good as ours.

I mean, no one *else* had a poodle modelling for them!

"The dog is *great*," Georgie said to me, during the last few minutes of getting organized.

Ally's mate Billy was just lifting Precious – kitted out in his stripy leg warmers – up on to the stall. Who knew how long Precious would stay there shivering and looking cute (Ally promised to feed him doggy treats as a bribe), but hopefully long enough for the mayor to come by during his judging.

But it wasn't just the stall and the dog that made our presentation stand out – it was also the cardboard-box-a-thon (my last-minute, inspirational idea).

I held my (good) hand out to help Georgie clamber into *her* box.

"So what time are you going to go off to that fairy thing?" she asked, stepping a second trainered foot inside.

"I'm not," I told her. "I've got no one to take me there."

"Oh! But you really wanted to go! You wanted to try to meet up with that girl from your school!"

She meant Libby-Mae Ferguson, of course.

"Nah," I said bleakly. "She turned into a *frog*. . ."

I could sense poor, confused Georgie staring at me, trying to figure out what I meant. But *I* spoke before *she* did.

"He's doing that staring thing again," I said under my breath, aware of Marlon – in his own box – boring his eyes into the side of my head. "Wish he wouldn't do that!"

"It's only because he fancies you!" announced Georgie.

Ha!!!!! She really *was* confused.

Before I could set her straight, someone spoke directly to me in a very forceful way.

"We're from the *Hornsey Journal*," said a smartly dressed girl with a notepad, as she pointed to a beardy bloke with a camera. "So what exactly are you doing here with all these boxes?"

"Well, we're calling it a cardboard-box-a-thon," I explained, clambering into my own box, as the Saturday morning Crouch End shoppers milled out of the supermarket opposite and came over to see what on *earth* was going on with all those stalls and those eight kids randomly standing still inside a bunch of empty old boxes.

"And what does it represent?" asked the girl reporter, scribbling furiously away.

"It represents how ALL of us are personally responsible for the rubbish we create," I told her, as the photographer's camera loomed in closer for a snapshot of me and my sweetie wrapper hair clips and my pink plaster cast. (Yikes!)

"Mmmm, interesting. . ." muttered the girl, still scribbling. "Now can you tell me your friends' names, for the caption we'll print with the picture?"

My heart suddenly went BOOM, as I thought of us all about to be famous(ish), with a feature perhaps right next door to one of the freebie competitions I'd been entering the last few weeks!

(Wonder if I'll win the slug pellets from last Friday's edition?!)

"Well, *she's* Georgie," I said, pointing first to my very own buddy, who was grinning proudly, but with her face as Arsenal red as her top.

I suddenly paused before I got on to the rest of the gang, feeling a little teary gulp get in the way of everyone's names.

OK, so maybe we *were* an oddball-geek group: from out-there William (who'd insisted on sitting in his box with the flaps closed) to tiny Bianca (who could hardly see out of her box – but then we had given her the biggest 'cause it was funny); from grinning Omar to Verity, who was thankfully *not* eating her hair for the photo; from me with my pink ribbony plaits and matching plaster cast to Marlon the champion starer; from earnest Yusuf back to Georgie the shy-girl tomboy.

And in our own unique, oddball, geeky way, we were FANTASTIC!

"Exemplary!!" the mayor agreed, looking over all our efforts and handing a big red winners' rosette to Miss Boyle. (Good use of vocabulary, your honour!!)

"What a *team*!" Miss Boyle high-fived us as we clambered out of our boxes.

I watched as Georgie punched the air, like she'd scored a goal.

Georgie, who'd started off silent and shy and who'd been more likely to wear a cardboard box over her *head* when I first met her. I guess being in our oddball/geeky group had helped her confidence a bunch.

And maybe knowing me a little had helped her too, I guess, even if that just meant she'd learned how to secretly stand up to bullies with a sewing needle!!!

Actually, there I was, thinking that the Find Your Inner Fairy website had been the only truly sparkly, special thing in my life these last few weeks, when hanging out with all these guys and getting to know Georgie had been pretty sparkly and special too. . .

Grinning at the sight of Georgie and Miss Boyle and the others, I didn't think I could feel any happier, till someone tapped me on the shoulder and shouted: "HEY, CINDERELLA!! GUESS WHERE *YOU'RE* GOING?"

The shouter was Linn, who happened to be standing holding a big IKEA bag that had the tip of a glittery fairy wing sticking out of it.

"Who's *she*, then?" Marlon asked me, with a nod towards Linn.

"LET'S JUST CALL ME HER FAIRY GODMOTHER," said Linn, shooting him a look.

She was my Fairy Godmother all right.

And who needs a pumpkin coach and horses to whisk you to the Fairy Fun Day Ball, when a responsible nearly-sixteen-year-old big sister and a No. 91 bus will take you straight there?!?

Saturday 2.35 p.m.

Oh, it's all so beautiful, *beautiful*, BEAUTIFUL!!!

I have *never* seen so much colour and glitter and twinkling and sparkle in my life!

Everywhere I look, there are *hundreds* of fairies: beautiful fairies; fat fairies; goth fairies; fluffy fairies; bloke fairies; kiddie fairies; old fairies; fairy babies . . . I've even seen a hairy fairy *dog* with a mini set of wings and a flashing collar.

There have been fairies dancing on the stage and soggy fairies dancing through the Trafalgar Square fountains.

There are balloons and streamers everywhere, and multicoloured fairy dust (bought from the fairy-dust kiosk) being chucked by the handful in the air.

Am I in a dream and secretly sleepwalking again?!

Nope, it's all *100%* for real; I know this because I got some turquoise fairy dust in my eyes a second ago and it nipped quite a lot. . .

Right now, I'm resting my fairy wings (accessorized with my skating net skirt) by sitting cross-legged in front of the Find Your Inner Fairy Information Stand.

Linn has gone to find drinks from somewhere (it's thirsty work being a teenage fairy, and a teenage fairy's reluctant escort). She says she'll get on faster by herself, and that I'm a liability, what with my home-made wings banging into every other fairy's wings every five seconds.

She's left me to flutter (ha, ha!) on my own here by the Find Your Inner Fairy Information Stand, and has warned me that if I move ONE step away from it, she will personally pull off my fairy wings "AND WRAP THEM AROUND YOUR NECK".

But even though Linn's sceptical face and plain clothes make her stand out like a carrot in a meringue shop, I am SO grateful to her for taking me here.

And I'm SO grateful for Grandma phoning Linn this morning while she was on her way to meet her old friends for tea and cake to persuade my big sis to do it.

And I'm SO grateful to Dad for phoning Grandma late last night to ask her advice about what to do about me and my desperation to go to the Fairy Fun Day.

And I'm SO grateful to Ally, who tiptoed into Dad's room last night to tell him that he HAD to find some way of letting me come today.

(Can you believe Ally – *she's* like my very own eleven-year-old fairy godmother!)

Wow, it's all so *magical* – apart from the paving stones I'm sitting on, which are quite uncomfy – that I can hardly breathe.

Maybe I should take a few deep breaths.

I must be hyperventilating.

'Cause it's as if there's a delicate shower of rose-pink fairy dust drifting down in front of my eyes. . .

Saturday 6.32 p.m.

We got home about five minutes ago, me and Linn and a handful of gold fairy dust that I sprinkled *whoosh!!* in the air, right over our front garden, with a flurry of it landing on Mr and Mrs Misery-Guts' begonias.

Ha!

Maybe it'll work its magic on the two of them?! (I doubt it – Mr and Mrs Misery-Guts have got double-wrapped tinfoil around their hearts. Plus they're very old, and tutting at me seems to be an enjoyable hobby for them. Maybe it would be cruel of me to wish it away from them?)

But what a day, what a day, what a DAY.

!!!

By the way, I wasn't imagining the rose-pink shower, when I was curled up under the Find Your Inner Fairy Information Stand.

Someone was *deliberately* sprinkling it down on me.

"Well, fancy meeting *you* here, Rowan Love!!" said a

smiley voice, when I looked up to see where it was coming from.

The face that matched the smile was round and friendly, with rosebud lips and brown bobbed hair crowned with a hoop of entwined ivy leaves, red berries and something that might have been hazelnuts.

"Miss Boyle?!" I squeaked, scrambling up to my feet.

"Oh, I'm off-duty here!!" laughed Miss Boyle, resplendent in a red chiffon, pointy-edged mini-dress. "I'm just a regular common-or-garden fairy now! Sacha Fairy, actually! Pleased to meet you!!"

As she gently shook my quivering hand, my mind whipped back to a glitter-covered flyer on the library floor a few weeks ago, when our oddball-and-geeks group had our first meeting with Miss Boyle. I'd thought Libby-Mae Ferguson had dropped it, but it must have been *her* . . . Miss Boyle, I mean.

Sacha Boyle.

Sacha *Fairy* Boyle, of the Find Your Inner Fairy website!!!!!!

Who knew I had a real live *fairy* as a teacher?!

"Oh! I wrote to you!" I said dumbly.

"I know!" she giggled.

"Did you realize it was me?" I said, even more dumbly.

"Well, *yes*, Rowan, because Rowan Love's a pretty unique name!"

What – unique as it *is*? Without any interesting and memorable middle name?!

"But if you knew it was *me*, why didn't you just say it was *you*?" I asked her.

I worried that my panic goblin was beginning to pitter-patter in my chest, but the feeling was too fluttery. Maybe it was my inner fairy, finally stretching her wings!

"Rowan, you were taking a real risk, and breaking some important fundamental safety rules by writing to me," said Miss Boyle, trying to look like a stern teacher for a second, which was tricky, since she was dressed in twinkly red-and-brown wings which were *boinging* behind her as she leant on the table to talk to me. "I tried very hard to set you straight about that. And there was no way I was going to encourage you."

"But there *was* something written on the blog. . ." I muttered, thinking about the "*be your own best friend*" line in particular.

Miss Boyle crinkled her nose in an admission of guilt.

"Well, I *might* have told Jacqui, who runs the website,

about you, and asked her to write some kind of vague but positive message on there."

"Thanks." I smiled at her shyly, not quite believing I wasn't dreaming all this fairy dust and fantastic-ness. "Um . . . by the way, is Jacqui Fairy your *sister* or something?"

"Jacqui?! No!!" Miss Boyle grinned. "I just met her at a music festival when I was a student, and fell in love with her fairy stall. I've been helping her out ever since!"

"Oh," I mumbled, realizing that I'd made stuff up to fit again, just like I had with Libby-Mae Ferguson, when I'd wanted her to be dazzlingly magical, instead of deeply normal, with added obnoxious bits.

If I had any room left on the Raspberry Rules list (which I don't), I could've definitely added Rule No. 19: *I will NOT jump to conclusions. . .*

"So have you come here with a friend today?" asked Miss Boyle, gazing around to see whoever I'd fluttered here with.

"My sister brought me down. I'm pretty best-friend free, remember?"

"You'll find another one," said Miss Boyle, patting my hand reassuringly. "People with lots in common tend to stumble across each other eventually, so be patient!"

As soon as she said that, I realised something kind of *shocking*: me and Erin had hardly *anything* in common. I mean, we both loved movies, but that was *one*-thing-in-common versus about a-zillion-*nothing-much-in-commons*.

Were we ever – gulp – *properly* best friends?

Or just two people who accidentally got together and just bumbled along for a bit 'cause there was no one else around?!

Maybe Grandma and Ally sort of *knew* that all along . . . it would make sense of what they'd each said this week; i.e., "Who needs enemies with friends like that!" (Grandma) and "Easily!" (Ally, when I'd wondered aloud how I could ever replace Erin).

"And in the meantime," Miss Boyle trilled on, while my mind whirred, "just chill out with people who you feel comfortable to be around. I'm sure there are plenty of them!"

I was about to say no, there wasn't anyone really, when I stopped. 'Cause like Fluffy, I don't *have* to be on my own.

When it comes to people I feel comfortable with, there's always Ally (my little fairy god*sister*).

And Dad and Grandma and Tor, of course . . . and even Linn, though she likes to pretend I'm as annoying as being stung by a jellyfish.

And now I know William and Marlon and Verity.

I mean, they've all got their own friends (well, William and Marlon seem teamed up as best mates now, and Verity had her own crew of giggly girls). I'm pretty sure all of them will *always* think I'm a bit strange, and I can't see me and Verity bonding over hair-chewing, but, yeah, that wouldn't stop them all from being people I can hang out with at break times and lunch hours, and moan about Mrs Wells banning my flip-flops or whatever. Just as long as Marlon stops that stupid *staring* thing. . .

Then there's Georgie.

I mean, who says a glitter addict like me can't be mates with a shy-ish football fan history nut? We could have stuff in common! Maybe Georgie can explain football and the fall of the Third Reich to me sometime, and I can try and persuade her to let me plait red ribbons in her hair to match her Arsenal tops!!

"Miss Boyle, can I ask you something?" I said in a rush, as a question suddenly flapped into my head.

"Ask away!" replied Miss Boyle, throwing her hands to the side and releasing a sprinkling more of rose-pink fairy dust.

"Did you pick us for your project – me and William

and Marlon and Verity, I mean – because we were all a bit . . . *weird* in our own way, and you felt sorry for us or something?"

Miss Boyle gave a short, loud laugh and pointed to herself.

"Do you think someone who dresses like *this* and encourages people to be *fairies* for a hobby would feel sorry for people being *weird*?!" she giggled, making her hand-painted wings jiggle madly. "Rowan, I asked Mrs Wells to help me find some creative and interesting people, who maybe didn't get a chance to show their potential at school because they were overshadowed for some reason. Does that make sense?"

Yes; it made mad, beautiful, fairy-tale sense to me.

And I spent the rest of the afternoon dancing (on stage and in the fountains), sketching (all shapes and sizes of fairies) and scampering (under every shower of fairy dust being thrown in the air).

"WOULDN'T WANT TO BE THE STREET CLEANERS SWEEPING *THAT* OFF THE PAVEMENTS IN THE MORNING!!" Linn growled as we stepped on the No. 91 bus back home.

I didn't see it myself – they normally have to deal with yucky stuff like sticky drinks cans and cigarette butts and dog poo in their daily job, so I'm sure the street cleaners of central London will be out at six tomorrow morning with smiles on their faces a mile wide as the early-morning sun spangles on a rainbow of fairy glitter and—

CRUNCH!!

The pneumatic doors of the bus closed *right* on my left wing, bending it in half.

Linn looked at me sharply, thinking I was going to *cry*, probably.

But instead I started giggling, 'cause *now* I matched Libby-Mae Ferguson's wonky-winged brooch! (Which *isn't* still languishing in the bin of the Female Visitors' Toilets, by the way; I rescued it as soon as I got out of Mr Svenson's class. It's Blu-tacked in the back of this journal, keeping my inner fairy company and causing a strange lump in the pages.)

I curled up on the back seat of the bus (well, as much as you can curl with wings on) and smiled to myself all the way home, my head full of raspberry glitter instead of Raspberry Rules. . .

OK; I'm going to stop scribbling all today's delicious dramas in my journal for now.

Think I'll go downstairs and confuse Linn some more (yay!) by sitting at my toy laptop and pretending to write some make-believe emails.

I fancy writing one to Mum saying, *"Hi, I love you, wherever you are."*

And then one to my future best friend (wherever she is now) to say, *"Hi, I'm looking forward to meeting you!"*

Whoever she is (Georgie, maybe?) I hope that my future best friend doesn't mind someone who is disorganized and unfocused and rambles a lot, because that's who I am.

And you know something?

I think that's *maybe* all right. . .

SIX WEEKS LATER (OOPS...)

Greetings!

I'm writing this in the toilets.

Not the Female Visitors' Toilets at school (they closed to scuzzy students *forever* ago), but the loos in Wood Green Cineworld.

We're here 'cause I won a competition (in the *Hornsey Journal* of course) for a VIP trip for six to the cinema to see *Beverly Hills Baboon*.

!!!

Pretty good, eh?

The "we" is me, Dad, Linn, Ally, Tor and Georgie, though technically Linn isn't here any more (she only wanted the ride-in-the-stretch-limo part, and now she's gone to meet her mates somewhere cooler than a PG-rated film about a red-bottomed monkey), and Dad has fallen asleep in his popcorn (it's been a busy Saturday for bike repairs).

Wow . . . you should have *seen* Georgie's mum's and little sisters' faces when we pulled up in the limo outside her flat – there was just a blur of pink and squealing on her balcony!!

"Oh. It just feels like a long car with a sofa in it," Georgie said in surprise, when she clambered in. (True fact: stretch limos are a *lot* less exciting inside than you think they'll be. Ally said she expected something fancier, like automatic M&M dispensers. Tor thought there might be a *pool*. Still, he liked it when the driver pressed a button and Dad got to wave Mr Penguin out of the sunroof.)

Anyway, I've come to the toilets because a sad bit in the film made me choke up a little, and I thought I'd sneak off rather than scare Tor and everyone else by openly snivelling.

Here's what got me: the baboon is in this rich Hollywood guy's private zoo, and it's become friends with his daughter, who has to go off to boarding school or whatever. And it was just as the baboon and the kid hugged bye-bye that I remembered that *I'll* be hugging *Georgie* bye-bye in a few days' time.

Can you believe my luck? After the recycling project ended, I started to hang out with Georgie *loads*, and had just begun to think that we could *definitely* be best friends (she got to know all the lyrics to *The Sound Of Music*) – when it turns out her whole family is moving to an army base in Germany to be closer to her soldier dad. !?!?!?

Still, I think Georgie will do OK.

I gave her Miss Boyle's advice about being patient when it comes to meeting new mates, and being your own best friend in the meantime (© the Find Your Inner Fairy website).

Then I pointed out to Georgie that she's quite a bit more chatty and chilled-out than she used to be (which kind of helps when you're getting to know people!), AND her Arsenal football shirts will be a cool talking point in a land of Bayern Munich supporters, I guess.

I pointed out too that she is very intuitive. Can you believe she was right about *Marlon*? I found out the week after the Fairy Fun Day. I'd turned up at school with the knitted fairy wings I'd made for Fluffy fastened at the back of my hair, and he took one look at me and said, "You know something, Ro? I could *almost* fancy you, but you're just that bit *too* weird. . ."

Still, he's a sort of friend and said it with a grin, so I didn't take offence.

By the way, I know it's really rubbish that I haven't written in this journal for six whole weeks. I think the problem is that I have the attention span of Graham the Snail (either versions one *or* two*).

The trouble was, the night of the Fairy Fun Day, I lay awake – just me, Fluffy and a skin-covering of luminous multicoloured fairy dust – and stared at the Raspberry Rules in my big gold frame.

Suddenly *all* I could see (if I crossed my eyes and made everything a bit fuzzy) was a whole bunch of "*will NOT!!*"s, "must *ALWAYS!!*"s, "*NEVER!!*"s and "*PAY ATTENTION!!*"s, which didn't seem very fluffy or fun all of a sudden.

Maybe the problem was that I figured that out of eighteen rules, I had only managed to stick to *three*:

- Raspberry Rule No. 11 (*I will NOT put raspberries in soup*),
- Raspberry Rule No. 12 (*I will NOT eat emergency sandwiches over my journal while reading through it*) and . . .
- Raspberry Rule No. 13 (*I will NEVER put rubbish out while only wearing out-of-date pants and a tartan blanket*).

Otherwise, I'd failed them all spectacularly.

I've even broken an *easy* one, i.e., No. 16: *I will NOT*

drop journals or important documents in the bath, as you might be able to see from the wonky corner there. (Though I *did* leave it under a pile of heavy magazines and a snoozing Fluffy to try to flatten it out again.)

So anyway, in the light of my general uselessness, I came to decide some *extremely* important things.

Oh, yes.

I am going to . . .

1) leave the journal writing to my much more grown-up and dependable younger sister Ally,
2) keep this journal mostly for doodling and design purposes only from now on,
3) paint over ALL the impossible-to-keep Raspberry Rules in pure brilliant white (got some in the shed), and hang something new and cute inside my gold frame instead (possibly the full-page report of the recycling exhibition from the *Hornsey Journal*, starring me, Georgie, Marlon and everyone!),
4) come up with one *new*, simple Raspberry Rule, which is (No. 1-and-only) *Be happy* (hey, it's so easy to remember, I don't have to write it down anywhere!), and . . .
5) donate my pink plaster cast to Tor's latest rescue gerbils as a fun run, now that it's been cut off.

And THAT is my absolute, *final* word!!

Goodbye (think glittery thoughts)...

Rowan (no middle name) Love xxx

P.S. Grandma got me a mirrorball at a car boot sale at the church down the road from hers. It's EXCELLENT!

P.P.S. Went into that second-hand record shop in Crouch End earlier today and – get *this*! – a kind of goth/grunge girl and her pure grunge boy buddy started talking to me! It was 'cause they completely *loved* my old-lady beady rucksack.

Then we talked for a bit about what music we liked and stuff (they'd both heard of Kate Bush!!), and the girl (who is called Von) said we (i.e., her mate Chezza too) could maybe meet up next Saturday in the Hot Pepper Jelly Café and have an Americano and trail round the shops together after!!

It's SO exciting, and *maybe* the start of something?! I just need to find out what an Americano is first... (A kind of cake? A sort of hot-dog sandwich?)

* Tor snuggled up to me on the sofa last night and let Graham the Snail Take Two slither all over this journal. (Tor thinks it's amazing that Graham can do a wiggly line. I think Graham might just have the snail equivalent of glue ear and have compromised balance, personally.)

Anyway, Tor hit me with a biggie, in the tiniest of cosy whispers: "I KNOW this is a *different* Graham, Ro. I knew straight away by the swirls on his shell. I just didn't want to tell you I knew, in case you got upset. . ."

Isn't my little brother the *cutest*? I'm SO going to make him a mini memory shrine, in honour of Graham the Snail Take One!

Just got to go and dig his shell up out of the garden as soon as we get home from the cinema. . .